Outside the Gate

DENNIS,

JUST MAKING SURE
YOU HAVE SOMETHING
TO READ — HERE'S
ANOTHER.

ALL THE BEST,

TOM

Outside the Gate

Tom Milton

NEPPERHAN PRESS, LLC
YONKERS, NY

Published by Nepperhan Press, LLC
P.O. Box 1448, Yonkers, NY 10702
nepperhan@optonline.net
nepperhan.com

PUBLISHER'S NOTE
This is a work of fiction. Names, characters, places, and incidents
are the product of the author's imagination or are used fictitiously,
and any resemblance to actual persons, living or dead, events, or
locales is entirely coincidental.

Printed in the United States of America

Library of Congress Control Number: 2012922376

ISBN 978-0-9839412-7-9

Cover art was licensed from Publitek, Inc.

For Marie

Outside the gate there are vicious dogs
and tricksters and traffickers and murderers
and money worshippers and pathological liars.

Revelation 22:15

St. Anselm, 2012

ONE

WHEN SHE LEFT the girls playing tennis Carol had no reason to worry about them. The tennis pro was watching them and giving them advice. The court was visible from the hotel room, close enough so that she could hear their cries of glee and their groans of dismay. The Royal Palms was enclosed by a high wall, with only one gate that allowed people to come and go. And since the resort provided everything, including meals and drinks and various types of recreation, there was no reason for guests to go outside the gate.

"You're not tired?" she asked Amanda before leaving them. The girls had played three sets of doubles with her and Brian, then two sets of singles with each other.

"I'm not tired," Amanda said.

"I'm not either," Stacy said.

They were twelve years old, with seemingly unlimited energy. They were also best friends, so if one wasn't tired the other couldn't be.

"Okay," Carol said. "Play one more set, and then come in."

"We will. Don't worry," Amanda said. She smiled, not shy about the braces that had recently been installed in her mouth.

"It's your serve," Stacy said, walking around to the other side of the net.

Carol lingered to watch her daughter serve, delighting in the way Amanda bent her knees before stretching up to hit the ball. She admired Amanda's form at tennis, having taken up the game herself only five years ago so that they could play as a family. Where she had grown up they didn't play tennis.

With a flash of metal from her gritted teeth, Amanda swung her racket and propelled the ball into the area where Stacy was waiting to receive it. Stacy returned it, and Carol left the girls rallying, satisfied that they were fully occupied.

It was their third day at the Royal Palms, and by now the girls had tried everything, but they didn't seem to have tired of anything. They even got up by nine in the morning.

Brian had gone a few steps ahead of her, and now she caught up with him and went with him to their room. The girls had an identical room next to them, with a king-sized bed on which they frolicked. This morning Carol had to remind them that the bed wasn't a trampoline.

In their absence the maid had straightened up the room and had left the air conditioning higher than Carol liked, so she went to the regulator and turned it down before she began to undress. In the meantime Brian had stripped to his bikini underwear and laid his sweaty clothes on a chair. He was still trim, with good definition in his abdominal muscles and not a trace of lover's handles.

"Go ahead," she told him. Since he didn't spend much time in the shower, she always let him go first, and then she could have her shower at leisure.

"I won't take long," he said, stepping out of his underwear.

She watched him stroll into the bathroom, aroused by the sway of his compact buns. At this point she was glad that the girls were on the tennis court and not in their room, where at any moment they might decide to come next door.

While Brian took his shower she peered out the window and saw the girls playing, with the pro watching them. At ease she pulled the gauzy curtain across the window and removed her bra and finally stepped out of her panties.

She was naked when Brian came out of the bathroom wearing one of the waffle-weave robes the hotel provided. From his eyes she could tell he liked what he saw, and without hesitation he came to her, opening the robe and wrapping it around her.

Later, though she wanted to remain next to him, she made herself get up and put on the robe and walk to the window. The girls were no longer on the tennis court, and assuming they had played one more set and then come in as they had been told, she went into the bathroom and took a shower, not spending as much time as usual.

As she dried herself she listened for the sound of the shower next door, but she didn't hear it. She was used to nagging Amanda to take showers since for some reason hygiene wasn't a high priority for girls that age, so she would have to go next door and make sure they both took showers. They were probably lying on the bed now, watching television.

With her hair still wet she got into her khaki shorts and pulled on a yellow top and told Brian: "I'm going to see what the girls are up to."

"Okay," he said, lying contentedly on the bed.

She went out and stopped at the door to the girls' room and knocked softly, conscious of the possibility that other guests might be napping at this hour.

When they didn't respond she knocked a bit harder, calling: "Amanda?"

There was still no response.

"Amanda? Stacy? If you're in there, please answer me." She couldn't open the door since each girl had her own electronic key, and the hotel had given them two keys for that room, which should have been enough.

They evidently weren't in the room, so Carol went back to her room, where she found Brian still lying where she had left him.

"They're not in the room," she told him.

"They're probably at the snack bar," he said, getting up. "I'll go and find them."

"Do you remember if they had their phones?"

"They always have their phones."

"Then I'll text them," she said, going to her handbag where she kept her phone. They had service on the island, so the girls were able to text each other and their friends at home, though Carol had asked them to control themselves since she knew there would be roaming charges. Texting was the only sure way of

3

getting a response from girls their age, so she had learned how to do it. She took out her phone and turned it on and went to her last conversation with Amanda and typed the message: "Amanda, where are you?"

Since her daughter was always checking for messages, Carol expected to get a response within a few minutes, so she watched the screen of her phone and waited for a message. When one finally appeared it said: "Call failed."

"It says the call failed," she said. "What does that mean?"

"It means there's no service," Brian said. By now he was dressed and ready to go.

"I have service. I see four bars, which is more than I usually see at home."

"That doesn't mean Amanda has service."

"But she can't be more than a few hundred feet away from here."

"Well, phones are tricky. They do strange things. I'll go and find them."

"I'll go with you," Carol said, beginning to worry.

They went out, and just to make sure that the girls weren't in their room they knocked on the door.

"Amanda?" Brian yelled at high volume. "If you're in there, please answer me."

A door across the hall opened a crack and a reedy male voice said: "Could you keep it down? We're trying to sleep."

Brian silently mouthed a curse word.

"They're not in there," Carol said. "If they were, they would have answered us."

Instead of waiting for the elevator, they took the stairs down to the ground floor, and they headed for the snack bar, where the girls liked to hang out. It was on a terrace overlooking the pool, and it had a roof of woven palm leaves that provided shade and local color.

The girls weren't there, but two teenage boys who had been playing tennis on the other court were sitting at a table.

"Hey, guys," Brian said. "Did you see the two girls who were playing next to you?"

"You mean the redhead and the blond?" one boy said.

"Yeah. Were they here?"

"No. At least they weren't here when we got here."

"Did they stop playing before you did?"

"I don't know. I guess they did."

"Did you notice where they went?"

"No. We weren't paying attention to them."

"They're too young for us," the other boy said.

"Do you remember how long ago they stopped playing?" Carol asked.

"I guess it was about a half hour ago."

"It was more than a half hour ago," the other boy said. "We've been here for a half hour."

"Well, it wasn't as much as an hour ago," the first boy said.

"So the girls stopped playing between a half hour and an hour ago?" Brian asked.

"Yeah," the boys said almost together.

"Let's go and talk with the tennis pro," Carol suggested.

"He should be able to tell us something," Brian agreed.

They walked around the pool and over to the tennis court, where they found the pro giving a lesson to a girl who looked younger than Amanda. He was standing in midcourt, hitting balls softly to her backhand.

"Excuse us," Brian said as they stopped at the sideline. "Can we interrupt you for a minute to ask you something?"

"Sure," the pro said. He had curly blond hair and placid blue eyes and a tan from being in the sun every day. Obligingly he walked over to them.

"You remember the girls who were playing singles after we left here?"

"Yeah, I was watching them and giving them advice."

"Can you tell us when they stopped playing?"

After pausing to think, the pro said: "It was before I started the lesson with this girl. So it was at least a half hour ago."

"Did you notice where they went?"

"Yeah. They went to the hotel. I assumed they were going to their room."

"They're not in their room," Carol said.

"Did you check the snack bar?"

"They're not there."

"Well, maybe they went to the computer room."

"That's an idea," Brian said. "They could be playing games there."

"Thanks," Carol said, taking out her phone. Again she texted her daughter, and again she got the message: "Call failed."

"No response?" Brian asked her.

"It said the call failed. Would it say that if Amanda had turned off her phone?"

"It might, but usually it would ask you to leave a message."

As they walked back around the pool, where people were still lying on the lounge chairs, trying to catch the last rays of sun, Carol already blamed herself for taking her eyes off the girls while she and Brian made love. She should have stayed at the tennis court and watched them. But they should have been safe there with the pro watching them. And whatever they were up to, they should be safe. A main reason why they were staying at this resort, which cost almost three hundred dollars per person per day, was that the girls would be safe here.

When they entered the computer room she saw only a lone boy playing an action game. The sight of this boy with his eyes fixed on a computer screen when he could have been swimming or playing on the beach reminded Carol of why she hadn't let the girls bring their computers. There were so many other things to do at the resort. Yet at this point she would have been thankful to find the girls playing on computers.

"Were two girls here?" Brian asked the boy.

Intent on maximizing his kill of aliens, the boy acted as if he hadn't heard Brian,

"I asked you if two girls were here."

"I didn't see them," the boy said without interrupting his concentration.

"Thanks," Brian said with irony that was lost on the boy.

"They might be on the beach," Carol said hopefully.

"Yeah, let's go and see," Brian said, putting his arm around her shoulder.

Carol appreciated this gesture of comfort, though it moved her closer to where she might need comfort.

They headed for the beach, scanning around them.

"They're here somewhere," Brian said with what still sounded like confidence.

"Unless they left the resort," Carol said, approaching the point where she was ready to consider this unlikely possibility.

"They have no reason to leave the resort. They have everything they could possibly want here."

"They might have wanted to see the island."

"We asked them if they wanted to go on a tour of the island, and they said they didn't."

"They might have changed their minds."

"Then they would have told us. They wouldn't have left the resort on their own."

She really didn't believe they would have. Amanda wasn't adventurous, and Stacy wasn't the kind of girl who would lead her astray. If Carol had had any doubts about Stacy she wouldn't have assumed responsibility for bringing her with them. So she couldn't imagine the girls leaving the resort on their own.

When they got to the beach they split and walked in opposite directions, Carol to the left and Brian to the right, in order to expedite their search. Though the sun was casting long shadows, there were still people in the green water, which was ideal for swimming since the bay was protected by a reef, and there were still children on the white sand, which wasn't ideal for building castles since it was so fine.

As she gazed at the ocean Carol had the sudden fear that the girls had gone swimming and gotten into trouble, but her fear was dispelled by the sight of two women more than a hundred feet out from the shore with the water only up to their thighs.

At the end of the bay was a rock jetty that not only protected the beach from erosion but also protected the Royal Palms from intruders, serving as an extension of the wall. It wasn't an impassable barrier, but it would have stopped all but the most determined intruders from coming in, and it certainly would have stopped the girls from going out.

Not seeing anyone except a couple in the deep shadow of the jetty, lying on a towel and languorously kissing, Carol turned and looked toward the other end of the bay, where she saw Brian looking toward her. Though he was far away, she could tell from his deflated posture that he hadn't found the girls.

By the time they came together where they had split they had independently arrived at the next step: to get into the girls' room.

As they walked quickly back to the hotel Carol hoped that the girls were playing hide and seek, as they had done when they were younger. She would open the door to their room and find them lying on the bed and looking pleased with themselves. She understood how hard it was for children to imagine what it was like to be a parent and worry about them, so she was more than ready to forgive them for giving her a scare.

When they got to the desk they asked the man behind it for an extra key to the girls' room.

"We're looking for our daughter and her friend," Brian explained, "and we think they might be in their room."

"If they are," the man said as if he didn't understand them, "why don't they let you in?"

"We don't know if they're in there. We want to find out."

The man picked up a phone and made a call. After talking for a few interminable minutes he hung up and said: "I'll have someone let you in."

Another man came and escorted them to the girls' room, which he opened with an electronic key. With a silent prayer Carol went into the room and looked at the bed, but she saw only the tangled sheets and Amanda's bear, whose name was Bo. "Amanda? Stacy?"

There was no response.

She looked around and saw their tennis rackets on a chair. "They must have come back here and then gone out. And I don't see any sign of their changing, so they must have been wearing the same clothes."

After a silence Brian asked: "Do you think they could have left the resort?"

"I don't know what to think," Carol said, though she was still inclined to reject the possibility. "But if they did, then someone must have seen them."

"You could ask at the gate," advised the man who had let them into the girls' room.

Going ahead of him, they left the room and went down the stairs and out the main entrance. A shuttle bus from the airport was stopped there to let out new arrivals, who looked as if they had traveled overnight.

She followed Brian around the bus and out to the gate, where a tall man in uniform was posted, ostensibly to make sure that only authorized persons and vehicles were allowed to enter the premises. On his left shoulder was slung a rifle, which Carol assumed was only for show. In her research she had found no mention of crime on the island.

"Can I help you?" the gatekeeper asked them, having come to attention.

"Well, I hope you can," Brian said. "How long have you been at the gate today?"

"I've been here since noon. I get off at eight."

"Did you see two girls leave the resort?"

"Two girls? How old are they?"

"They're twelve," Carol said impatiently. "Did you see them?"

"No," the man said, shaking his head. "I didn't see them. If I had, I would have stopped them. Girls that age shouldn't be wandering around this island on their own."

"Is there any chance they slipped by you?"

The man stopped to think. "Yes, there's a chance. I left my post for a few minutes to help a woman start her car. But it was only for a few minutes."

"Do you remember what time that was?"

"I think it was about an hour ago."

She looked at Brian, unable to imagine the girls hiding behind a car and waiting for a chance to slip by the gatekeeper.

"Was anyone else around then?" Brian asked.

"Yes, there was a boy washing a car."

"Is he still around?"

"He's over there," the man said, pointing across the parking lot toward a figure in the shadows.

"Thanks. We'll talk with him."

Before they left him the man said: "If they were my girls, I'd go out there and look for them. They could get into trouble."

By now Carol was sick with fear, though she was still hoping that the girls were safe inside the walls of the resort.

When they approached the boy he turned off the nozzle of the hose he was using to rinse a black Mercedes, and he smiled at them expectantly.

"We need your help," Brian told him. "Did you see two girls leave the resort?"

"Were they a redhead and a blond?"

"Yeah. Did you see them?"

"I did," the boy admitted. "I was washing a car, and I heard a sound, so I looked up, and I saw two white girls running away. They went out so fast I couldn't stop them."

"What kind of sound did you hear?" Carol asked, trying hard to understand the girls' behavior.

"I don't know. I guess it was the kind of sound kids make when they get out of school."

"Do you have any idea where they might have gone?"

The boy considered. "The main road goes through the cane fields and to the airport. There's nothing on it that you'd want to see. But another road goes into town, and if you wanted to see something, you'd take that road."

"Will you help us look for them?" Brian asked.

"Sure, I will," the boy said, nodding. "I know where kids hang out in town."

"We should get a security guard to go with us," Carol said.

"I'll go and get one," Brian said, turning. He headed back into the hotel.

The boy coiled the hose and dragged it over to a service area to put it away.

As she waited for the boy and her husband to return Carol was angry at her daughter for pulling this stunt and making her worry. She didn't get angry at her daughter often, but there were times when Amanda tried her patience, usually for not cleaning up her room, or not taking a shower, or not brushing her teeth after being repeatedly asked to. Carol had never understood why her daughter refused to do things that didn't require much time or effort. But now she began to wonder if Amanda's refusals were minor acts of rebellion.

"Those girls looked young," the boy said after returning. "How old are they?"

"They're twelve," Carol said.

He didn't say it, but she could tell he was thinking: "Girls that age shouldn't be wandering around this island on their own."

"How old are you?"

"I'm fifteen."

He was only a year older than her son Matthew, who was in Vermont now with the family of a friend, but he looked much older. "Do you go to school?"

"Sure, I do. I'm a freshman in high school."

"You said you know where kids hang out in town."

"I know all the places," the boy said with pride for having such knowledge. "But there aren't many. We should go first to the place that sells ice cream."

To get ice cream the girls didn't need to leave the resort, but they may have imagined that outside its walls there were more exciting flavors.

A few minutes later a yellow golf cart came rolling across the parking lot with Brian in front, next to a security guard. There were seats behind them, facing the rear, and when the cart stopped, Carol and the boy got on.

11

"Are you sure you want that boy to go with us?" the security man asked, peering at her through gray aviator sunglasses.

"He knows where kids hang out in town."

"Well, don't worry. We'll find them. My name is Derek."

They drove out the gate and after going a short distance they turned onto a road that wasn't as smoothly paved as the road to the airport, and they had to dodge potholes.

On the outskirts of town the houses were built with pieces of wood that looked as if they had been collected from different sources, and they were painted mostly blue and green. The roofs were metal, and there were no panes or screens on the windows.

"Do they have running water?" Carol asked the boy.

"No," the boy said. "They haul it from a well to their houses. But in town they have running water."

Confronted by the stark facts of poverty, she could understand why the bus from the airport hadn't brought the tourists through town. It would have marred the illusion of an island paradise. And if the girls had come this way, they would have been shocked. So why hadn't they fled back into the safety of the resort?

In the center of town the buildings were made of cinder block, and some of them had glass windows. But the town didn't seem to have any tourist attractions. It looked like just a place to live for people who worked at the Royal Palms.

Derek stopped the cart in front of a one-story building that was painted white and roofed with palm fronds. It didn't have glass windows, but inside it was clean and well-lighted, with tables and chairs painted bright blue.

Two little kids without their mother were sitting at a table, eating ice cream out of cups with white plastic spoons.

A plump woman greeted them from behind a counter, asking: "Can I help you?"

"We're looking for two girls," Brian told her.

"Were they white girls?"

"Yeah. A redhead and a blond."

The woman nodded. "They were here. We don't often see white girls here."

"How long ago did you see them?" Carol asked anxiously.

"About a half hour ago. They bought cones and then they left. I assumed they were in town with their mother."

While this last remark faulted her for letting the girls go into town on their own, the image of Amanda walking down the street with an ice cream cone, oblivious of what she was doing to her parents, made Carol even more angry at her daughter.

"Did you notice which way they went?" Brian asked.

"They went that way." The woman pointed in the direction away from the resort.

"Did you see them come back?" Derek asked her.

"No. I didn't," the woman said, shaking her head. "And I was beginning to wonder what happened to them."

"You were? Why?" Carol asked.

"Well, they couldn't keep going down this street. It ends at the harbor. So after a while they should have come back."

"Could they have come back another way?" Brian asked.

"They could have, but I don't know why they would have. There's nothing to see on the other streets."

"They could still be hanging out at the harbor," Carol said, hoping. "Stacy likes boats."

"There aren't many boats," the woman said. "There're some fishing boats, and usually a yacht. They've been talking for years about improving the harbor so cruise ships can stop here, but that'll never happen."

"Thanks," Carol said. "Let's go to the harbor."

They got back into the cart and continued down the street. For a while a dog that had been lying at the edge of the street trotted after them, but it finally gave up.

"Can you think of any other place they might have gone?" Carol asked the boy.

"No. But they're probably hanging out at the harbor. I used to hang out at the harbor. There wasn't much happening, but at least I could get away from my family."

13

Carol could understand why kids wanted to get away from their families, but she wished the girls had waited until they got back home.

It took them only a few minutes to arrive at the harbor, where they got out and looked around. An old pier extended out a few hundred feet, and several fishing boats were anchored beyond it. In the distance a boat was coming in, bucking the waves.

As they walked out onto the pier Carol looked around for the girls, but there wasn't any sign of them, and by now she was frantic with worry.

"They're not here," Brian said, stopping.

"Then where *are* they?" she asked desperately.

"They could have gone back another way," Derek suggested.

"So let's go back and look for them."

They were approaching the cart when the boy halted as if something had caught his eye. He leaped into the brush and retrieved it, saying: "It's a phone."

"Let me see it," Brian commanded.

The boy handed over the phone, which was visibly damaged.

"It's Amanda's phone," Brian said after checking for her mark of identification.

"Oh, God," Carol cried, taking the phone from him to have a closer look at it. She prayed that he was mistaken.

But it was Amanda's, and it hadn't been damaged accidentally. Someone had deliberately crushed it.

"I'll call the police," Derek said, pulling out his phone.

TWO

THOUGH IT SEEMED like it took them forever, the police arrived in less than ten minutes. They drove up in a white Toyota and stopped a few feet short of the pier. They wore khaki uniforms with short-sleeved tunics, open at the neck, with their rank insignias displayed on epaulettes. Their military hats were dark green with red bands.

The officer who had been riding in the passenger seat, a solid man with heavy brows and deep-set eyes, introduced himself as Inspector McGuire and his partner as Sergeant Wilson. Both officers greeted Derek as if he was a former colleague.

"Tell us what happened," McGuire said.

"We're staying at the Royal Palms," Brian said. "Our daughter and her friend were playing tennis, and for some reason they left the resort."

"How old are they?"

"Twelve."

McGuire grimaced as if he knew from experience what could happen to wandering girls on the island. "Derek told me you found a cell phone."

"Here," Brian said, showing it to the officer.

Without touching the phone McGuire inspected it. "It looks like someone stomped on this phone. Where did you find it?"

"Over there," the boy said, pointing.

"Is this your daughter's phone?"

"Yes," Carol said.

"How do you know?"

"We bought identical phones for our daughter and our son, and to tell them apart Amanda put a little dot of pink nail polish on the back of hers."

15

Carefully taking the phone by its edges, McGuire turned it over and nodded. "Okay. It's her phone. Now, where were the girls last seen by anyone?"

"At the ice cream store," Carol said.

"They bought cones," Brian said, "and then they walked in this direction."

"How long ago did they leave the store?"

"By now it's about an hour ago."

"So if they came here directly, they arrived here about three quarters of an hour ago. And that would be," McGuire said, checking his watch, "around four thirty."

"We arrived here around five," Brian said. "We looked for them, but we didn't see them."

"Other than the phone," McGuire asked Derek, "did you find any evidence that the girls were here?"

"No," Derek said. "But they must have left footprints."

"We'll look for footprints, and in the meantime we'll assume they were here."

"What do you think happened to them?" Carol asked, unable to wait for the police to go through their process.

McGuire took a long deep breath and slowly exhaled. "Based on what happened to this phone, I think they were assaulted."

"Why didn't they scream for help?" Brian asked.

"If someone pointed a gun at you and told you that if you made a sound he'd shoot you, would you scream for help?"

"You mean there are people on this island who have guns?"

"There are people everywhere who have guns."

Compelled to follow where the officer was going, Carol said: "So you think the girls were taken away from here at gunpoint?"

"I don't think they went away willingly," McGuire said. "But I don't know what happened. We need to find a witness."

"There was no one here when we arrived," Derek said.

"A boat just came in," Wilson said, looking up from the pad where he was taking notes.

"They wouldn't have been here at the time it happened," McGuire said, "but maybe they can tell us something."

16

Wilson called out to the boat, which now was anchored in the harbor. Though the fishermen obviously weren't ready to come in, he gestured to them in a way that ordered them to drop what they were doing and row their dinghy to the shore.

As they walked over to meet the fishermen McGuire asked: "Do you have any idea why the girls left the resort?"

"I guess they wanted to see the island," Carol said.

"They could have seen the island by going on a tour."

"They didn't want to go on a tour."

"You mean they wanted to go on their own," McGuire said as if he understood.

They stopped at the shore and waited for the dinghy, which Wilson helped the two fishermen pull up on the sand.

"What did you want us for?" one of them asked.

"We have two missing persons," McGuire told him, "and we're hoping you saw something that can help us find them."

"When did they go missing?"

"Around four thirty."

"At that time we were out at sea."

"I know," McGuire said, "but did you notice anything while you were coming in?"

"No, nothing unusual. We only saw that yacht going out."

"It comes and goes so often, we don't pay much attention to it," the other man said. "But it was going faster than usual."

"It was also keeping a greater distance from us," the first man added.

"Where was it heading?" McGuire asked.

"It was heading west."

"Who owns it?" Brian asked.

"Some Russians," McGuire said with enmity.

"There are Russians on this island?"

"They came here several years ago with a lot of money, and they built a big house, and they have business operations."

"What kind of business operations?"

McGuire frowned. "We believe they're involved in criminal

activities, but we've never been able to make a case against them. They have connections at a high level."

"You think they could have taken the girls?"

"I think they could have."

"For what purpose?" Carol asked, afraid to imagine.

"We believe they're involved in human trafficking," McGuire said. "But they couldn't have gone far, so we should be able to stop them. And if we find the girls on their yacht, we'll have all the evidence we need."

She leaned against Brian for support while McGuire called headquarters and asked them to put out an alert for the Russian yacht *Pikovaya Dama*. The order was to stop and search the yacht for the missing girls.

"Who will that order go to?" Brian asked.

"It'll go to the ships you deploy in this area."

"We deploy ships in this area?"

"Yes. In your war on drugs."

"But the girls could still be on the island," Carol said.

"They could be," McGuire said. "And we're going to look for them. We're going to turn over every stone. But I have a feeling they're on that yacht."

"Has this kind of thing happened before?"

"It hasn't happened with white girls. But every year a few of our black girls go missing."

"You mean those Russians take them?"

"We've never caught the people who take them," McGuire said, "so we don't know if the Russians are involved. But we know we're dealing with organized criminals."

"You said they built a house on the island," Brian said. "Will you go there and question them?"

"Oh, yes. I'll go there while you're at headquarters. We'll need all the information you can give us about the girls."

They rode in the back of the police car to the police station, an old building in the center of town that looked as if it went back to the colonial era. It was built of gray stone, with white window trim and the island's flag hanging from a pole at the second floor.

Since McGuire had called ahead and given him the basic facts of the case, the detective who would take over was waiting for them in the reception area. Casually dressed in khaki pants and a green polo shirt, he had a high forehead and astute eyes that gave the impression that they didn't miss anything.

"I'm Detective Inspector Ramsey," he told Carol, offering not only his hand to shake but also a dose of empathy.

"I'm Carol Delaney," she managed to say, "and this is my husband Brian."

"I'm sorry we met under these circumstances," Ramsey said. He took from Wilson the plastic bag containing Amanda's phone, which he passed to a young man in uniform who was standing by, and then he led them to an office.

"Please sit down," he said, indicating a rectangular table.

Carol and Brian sat down together on one side, with Ramsey opposite them.

"Is this your first visit to the island?" Ramsey asked.

"Yes," Carol said. "It's our first visit to the Caribbean."

"You're staying at the Royal Palms?"

"Yes." She watched as he made a note on a pad.

"The girls' names are Amanda and Stacy?"

"That's right. Amanda's our daughter, and Stacy's her friend."

"So their full names are Amanda Delaney and Stacy—"

"Walker." It didn't seem necessary to add that the Walkers were close friends, though that was intensifying the pain.

"How old are they?"

"Twelve."

"Do you have any pictures of them?"

"I have a lot of pictures," Carol said, taking out her phone. She went to the area where pictures were stored, and she found the ones she had taken on this trip. They were still in the phone's memory since she didn't want to incur roaming charges for sending them to her email. She opened a picture of Amanda and

Stacy in tennis clothes and handed the phone to Ramsey, saying: "I took this today."

Examining the picture, Ramsey said: "They look athletic."

"They are. They're both good at sports."

"Are these the clothes they were wearing when they left the resort?"

"Yes. They went back to their room, but they didn't change. At least there wasn't any sign that they changed."

"Then we'll use this picture to look for them," Ramsey said, taking out his own phone and calling someone. "We can blow it up and make copies."

A few minutes later the young man who had taken Amanda's phone in the reception area came and took Carol's phone, with instructions from Ramsey to enlarge the picture of the girls and make a hundred copies.

When the young man had left the office Ramsey said: "I know you went over all this with Inspector McGuire, but I need to establish the timeline as accurately as possible. So let's start with the last time you saw the girls."

Responding to his questions, Carol helped him reconstruct the sequence of events from when they left the girls playing tennis to when they found the damaged phone.

"Do you have other children?" Ramsey asked after pausing to review his notes.

"We have a son."

"Is he here with you?"

"No. He's with a friend's family, skiing in Vermont."

"Do Stacy's parents have other children?"

"They have another daughter."

Ramsey made some more notes and then paused again with his head bent over the pad.

"What do you think happened to them?" Carol asked, unable to wait for him to finish his analysis. She was hoping he would have a different theory than McGuire.

Ramsey raised his head and looked at her directly. "I agree with Inspector McGuire. Based on what happened to your daughter's phone, I think they were assaulted. But there are at least two possibilities. One is that the girls escaped and are hiding somewhere. The other is that they were taken off the island."

"You mean by the Russians?" Brian asked.

"They had the ability to take the girls off the island. And their yacht was seen leaving the harbor around the time when the girls went missing."

"If they have the girls, then you have to stop them."

"We put out an alert for their yacht. We should be able to stop them."

"In the meantime," Carol said, "will they abuse the girls?"

"I don't think so," Ramsey said, shaking his head. "They don't like white girls. They like our black girls."

"Then why did they take Amanda and Stacy?" Brian asked.

"They can sell them to people who like white girls."

"Oh, God," Carol said, feeling sick.

"I'm sorry," Ramsey said, "but I have to be honest with you. And I trust that you'll be honest with me. It's the only way we can work together."

Brian leaned forward, clenching his fists on the table. "Are you saying they might sell the girls for sex?"

"I'm saying they might," Ramsey said evenly, "if we don't stop them."

"You said there's a possibility that the girls escaped," Carol said, still rejecting the other possibility.

"I think there is. The girls are young, and they look athletic, so they should have been able to outrun those gorillas."

"If they got away," Brian said, "we would have seen them."

"Not necessarily. They could be hiding. And they don't know we're looking for them."

"Where would they hide?"

"When I was their age, or even younger," Ramsey said, "I used to hide in the cane fields. It's hard for people to find you in the tall grass."

"Then you'll look for them in the cane fields," Carol said.

"We'll look for them everywhere."

21

After a moment Brian said: "I know why we haven't heard from Amanda, but Stacy has a phone, so why haven't we heard from her?"

"They could have broken her phone too."

"We didn't find her phone."

"You didn't look for it," Ramsey said. "If your daughter's friend still had her phone, she would have used it by now."

At that moment there was a knock on the door, and Ramsey said: "Come in."

It was the young man who had taken the phones.

"They found something on the girl's phone," he told Ramsey. "In the recent calls she dialed a number at 4:32 pm today."

"That was about a half hour before we got to the harbor," Brian said.

"What number did she call?" Ramsey asked.

The young man read the number from a piece of paper.

"That's my number," Carol said. "But I didn't get a call from her at that time."

"They could have taken her phone and stomped on it before the call went through," Ramsey said. "But luckily the phone stored the information."

"So now you know exactly when the phone was damaged," Brian said.

"We also know when the Russian yacht left the harbor. So if those girls aren't on the island, we know how they got off it."

Looking at his watch, Brian said: "You put out the alert an hour ago. Shouldn't you have heard something by now?"

"When we put out the alert the nearest ship was about fifty miles north of here, and the yacht was heading west, with a lead of three quarters of an hour. Its cruising speed is about eighteen miles per hour, so it would have been about thirteen miles west of here when the nearest ship began to pursue it. So even on a direct course the ship would take at least an hour and a half to catch it. And it could take longer," Ramsey added.

"What can we do in the meantime?"

"You can go back to your hotel and wait. I'll have a man drive you there. If you don't mind, he'll take a look at the girls' room."

"No, we don't mind."

"If you hear anything," Carol said, "you'll call us right away?"

"I will. But, as I said, it could take a while."

At that moment the young man returned and handed Carol's phone to Ramsey, who gave it to her, saying: "We have to keep your daughter's phone. It's evidence."

"I understand."

He led them out of the office and engaged a man to drive them back to the hotel. Before letting them go, he said: "I won't tell you not to worry, but I can assure you we'll do everything humanly possible to find those girls."

"Thank you," Carol said. "Do you have children?"

"I have two girls. They're ten and twelve."

"Then you can imagine how we feel."

Ramsey nodded. "Yes. I can. And my heart is with you."

As they rode in the police car back to the hotel they were silent for a while, and then Carol said: "I feel like this is my fault. I never should have taken my eyes off them."

"I have the same feeling," Brian said.

"I never imagined that they'd leave the resort."

"I never imagined it either. It's not something Amanda would have thought of doing by herself."

"Or Stacy by herself. But when two girls get together—"

They were silent again, overcome by worry.

"What I don't understand," Brian said, "is why they allow a Russian mob to operate here."

"The officer said they have connections at a high level."

"Well, if we'd known about them, we wouldn't have come here. And if the word gets out, no one will come here. So the people at a high level have an interest in stopping them."

"Maybe they already have their money in Swiss banks, so they don't care."

"And it doesn't bother them where the money came from?"

"Evidently not, or they wouldn't have taken it."

"They should be shot," Brian said in anger.

Carol wished she could share his feeling, but she was stuck with her own feeling. Over and over she told herself that she never should have taken her eyes off the girls.

When they arrived at the hotel the police officer got a copy of the key to the girls' room, and they all went there. They looked around for possible clues, but other than the tennis rackets, which provided evidence that the girls had come back to their room before leaving the resort, they didn't find anything.

"Do they have computers?" the officer asked.

"Yes," Carol said, "but they didn't bring them on vacation. We wouldn't let them."

"So they only had cell phones?"

"Smart phones," Brian said wryly.

"Well, if you see anything that might be helpful," the officer said, "please let us know."

"We will. Thanks."

When the officer had left them Carol went over to the bed and picked up Bo, who had slept with Amanda since she was three. He had come with a plaid ribbon around his neck, which Carol had removed when it began to fray, and now he wore a navy blue Yankees tee-shirt with Derek Jeter's name and number on the back. After nine years of being carted around and clung to he still looked respectable. And he smelled like Amanda.

Holding the bear against her face, she sobbed uncontrollably.

Brian came over and put his arms around her, trying to comfort her. But the only thing that would have relieved her was a phone call from Ramsey, informing them that the girls had been found, and that they were all right.

Back in their room they didn't know what to do with themselves. It was after seven, but they didn't feel like eating anything. And since there was no way of distracting themselves from the situation, they didn't turn on the television. They finally just lay down on the bed, side by side, and waited in silence.

"When do you think we should call the Walkers?" Brian asked after a while.

"I think we should wait until we hear from Ramsey."

"What if he has nothing to report?"

"Then at some point we'll have to call them. But let's hope he has good news for us."

They fell into a silence again.

With her eyes closed, Carol went back along the chain of events to early December when they decided to take the children somewhere for spring break. They finally had money to pay for a vacation since Brian had won a competition to design an affordable housing project after years of mainly doing plans to remodel homes. They considered a number of destinations, looking for a place that both children would enjoy, and they decided on St. Anselm, which friends had recommended. Carol was about to buy the seven-day package at the Royal Palms when Matthew was invited to go skiing in Vermont with a friend's family. At first she resisted the idea, wanting to keep her family together, but she finally yielded to her son's pleas, not wanting to deprive him of a chance to ski at Stowe. The final piece fell into place when Amanda asked if she could invite her friend Stacy so she would have someone to play tennis with.

If Matthew had come with them, Carol wondered, would he and Amanda have left the resort? She couldn't think of a time when they had done anything like that together, so she was inclined to think they wouldn't have. Still, if she had denied Matthew a trip to Stowe, he might have felt like doing something rebellious, and since he was two years older than his sister, he could have easily influenced her. So Carol couldn't say for sure if her mistake had been to let Matthew go with his friend and to bring Stacy with them.

As she went back and forth along the chain of events she kept stopping at the point where she had taken her eyes off the girls, and she kept feeling that if only she hadn't invited Brian to make love with her, the girls wouldn't have slipped by her.

About an hour later they were still lying on the bed when the phone on the bedside table next to her suddenly rang.

She reached over and answered it, praying.

"Mrs. Delaney?" the deskman said in the island lilt. "Detective Inspector Ramsey is here to see you. Would you like to come down or should I send him up?"

"Please send him up."

"I will. Thank you."

"Ramsey's here," she told Brian.

"Then he must have heard something."

She got up from the bed and prepared herself for the worst, assuming that if Ramsey had heard something good he would have told her over the phone.

As if he sensed what she was thinking, Brian came to her and hugged her.

Then she hastily picked up the clothes that were lying on the chairs and dumped them on the bed so there would be a place for them to sit.

There was a knock on the door, and Brian opened it.

"It's better that we're meeting here," Ramsey said, standing in the doorway. "We'll have more privacy."

"Please come in," Brian said.

As soon as Brian had closed the door behind him, Ramsey said: "We heard from the ship that pursued the yacht. They caught it about a half hour ago. And the girls weren't on it."

Carol let out a sigh of relief. "Then they're still on the island."

"I hope they are. But we haven't found them."

"Did you look in the cane fields?"

"We looked in the cane fields, we looked in the town, and we looked on the beaches. There are still a few places they could be, but—" The detective made a gesture that indicated he wasn't optimistic about finding the girls on the island, and since they were still standing in the area between the door and the bed, within close range of each other, his open hands were right there in front of Carol's face.

"I don't understand," she said. "You said the girls weren't on the yacht."

"They weren't on the yacht when the ship caught it. But they could have been on it earlier. And they could have been transferred to another boat."

"You mean the Russians had another boat out there waiting for them?" Brian asked as if he didn't believe it.

"They have a network," Ramsey said. "They could have asked for another boat."

"But why would they have transferred the girls so soon?"

"They might have known we were after them."

"How would they have known that?"

Recalling what McGuire had said at the harbor, Carol asked: "Could they have heard from someone at a high level?"

"No," Ramsey said, shaking his head. "No one at a high level knew we were pursuing the yacht. But the Russians could have intercepted our communications."

"If someone in your government tipped them off," Brian said, "we're filing a complaint."

"You're welcome to file a complaint, but it wouldn't help us rescue the girls."

"What *would* help you?" Carol asked.

"Finding evidence that they were on the yacht. If we can develop a strong enough case against those gorillas, we can make them talk."

"Where's the yacht now?" Brian asked.

"It's on the way back here. It'll be in port within a half hour."

"Then you can look for evidence that the girls were on it."

"We intend to do that. But they'll have had a lot of time to destroy the evidence."

"Would you like to sit down?" Carol asked, suddenly feeling inhospitable.

After checking his watch Ramsey said: "Well, only for a moment. I want to be at the harbor when the yacht comes in."

He sat in one of the chairs at the table and Carol took the other, while Brian pulled up the chair from the desk.

"Don't you need a warrant to search the yacht?" Brian asked.

"We have a warrant. We got it before their lawyer found out what was happening."

"They have a lawyer?"

"They all have lawyers," Ramsey said acidly.

"If the girls were transferred to another boat," Carol asked, "do you have any idea where they could have been taken?"

"They could have been taken anywhere."

"You should put out an alert for them," Brian said.

"We did put out an alert for them. But we don't know what kind of boat we're looking for."

"But you know *where* to look for it."

"We know the general area. But the boat could be heading in any direction," Ramsey said, "so it's a large area."

"Well, eventually they'll have to go into a port."

"Eventually they will. And we'll be watching for them at every port within range. But there are a lot of ports within range."

"What if you don't find any evidence that the girls were on the yacht?" Carol asked.

"Then we won't be able to prove they were on it," Ramsey said. "But that won't prove they weren't on it."

"Are you still looking for them on the island?"

"Oh, yes. And we'll keep looking for them." Ramsey paused, and then he asked Brian: "What do you do for a living?"

"I'm an architect," Brian said. "But I'm not a famous one. I make a living by doing plans to remodel homes."

"I work at a college in fund raising," Carol said.

"So you don't have a lot of money," Ramsey said.

"Do you think the girls were kidnapped for ransom?"

Ramsey nodded. "They could have been. Does the other girl's family have a lot of money?"

"They have more money than we do," Brian said. "But they're not rolling in it."

"If the girls were kidnapped for ransom," Carol asked, "then how soon would we receive a demand for payment?"

"Within a day or so," Ramsey said. "The people who kidnap for ransom usually want to make a deal as soon as possible."

"We have to call the parents of our daughter's friend," Brian said. "We've been waiting until we knew something. Should we wait until you've searched the yacht?"

Ramsey considered. "If we find evidence that the girls were on it, then we'll know what happened to them. If we don't find any evidence, then we'll still be where we are now, with a lot of questions but no answers."

"How long will it take you to search the yacht?"

"I don't know. It could take all night."

"Then we should wait until the morning?"

"If you wait," Ramsey said, rising from the chair, "we might know more than we know now. But we won't know less. And in any case, the parents of your daughter's friend will have one less night of worrying."

"And maybe you'll find the girls on the island," Carol said, still hoping.

"Maybe we will," the detective said as if he hadn't ruled out the possibility. And then he left, telling them he would let them know as soon as he found out anything.

THREE

IT WAS THE longest night of Carol's life. For fear of missing a communication of any kind, they didn't leave their room. They paced the floor, they sat in the chairs, and they lay on the bed waiting to hear from Ramsey.

She tried to recall what she knew about the world when she was Amanda's age. She knew from experience on the streets of her neighborhood that people could be nasty and violent. She remembered making a detour around a crime scene where two men had held up a deli and killed the owner. And she remembered hearing a friend recount how she had been attacked by a man on the way home from school. She had been warned by her mother not to talk with strangers, and when she had a question about life, including sex, she asked her mother. Amanda never asked *her* mother about life since she could find answers to her questions on the internet. The kids who were Amanda's age relied on the internet for answers to their questions about life. They didn't need their mothers to explain how babies were made or to tell them what to expect as they went through adolescence. They acted like they knew everything, yet they knew less about the real world than their mothers had known at their age.

Aware of the distant sound of the ocean, Carol wondered what she could have said or done so that the girls would have known better than to leave the resort on their own. Should she have told them more about what happened in the world outside the gate? Would that have stopped them? Or would it have only made the prospect more enticing?

Around ten they ordered a ham sandwich and a soda from room service. It came on a tray with a linen napkin and tableware as well as a little pot of English mustard. Between the two of them they ate less than half of the sandwich, and Carol immediately wished she hadn't eaten anything since it hadn't gone down well.

By midnight they concluded that they wouldn't hear from Ramsey until morning, so they tried to get some sleep. But Carol was kept awake by thoughts of what would happen to the girls if the police didn't find them.

She prayed and prayed for their safe return, but her faith had never been tested before, and it was already wavering. It was hard enough to believe in a God who would torture her like this, and it was even harder to believe in one who would let girls be sold for sex.

The last time she had seen Amanda naked was after a recent battle to make her take a shower. At that time the only signs of puberty were her barely perceptible breast buds, which still didn't look much different than Matthew's. And there was no trace of pubic hair. So how would anyone get the idea of using her body for commercial purposes?

Repulsed by the possible fate of her daughter, Carol made it into the bathroom just in time to avoid ejecting the undigested bites of sandwich onto the floor.

She was standing at the window when the sun came up, and she wasn't cheered by the pink light that flowed across the ocean. It only meant that they wouldn't have to wait much longer to hear from Ramsey.

"How are you doing?" Brian asked. He was lying on the bed with his eyes wide open.

"Not well. I keep thinking—"

"Yeah. I know. I almost wish they hadn't told us about the Russians."

"They had to tell us sooner or later," Carol said, gazing out at the tennis courts. "And maybe it's better they told us while we still had hope."

"I still have hope."

"I do too. If I didn't have hope, I couldn't bear it."

"It's after six," Brian said after a long silence. "We should be hearing from Ramsey soon."

"I'm hoping they found no evidence that the girls were on the yacht. But if they did find evidence, we'd know what happened, and we'd have a trail."

"I'm still hoping they're on the island. But if they are, then why haven't the police found them? It's not a big island."

"Maybe they're being held hostage."

"Maybe they are. At least that wouldn't be as bad as the other possibility."

"No. It wouldn't," Carol agreed. "We could just pay money and get them back."

At that moment the phone rang.

"Mrs. Delaney?" the deskman said. "Detective Inspector Ramsey is here."

"Please tell him we'll come down and meet him in the lobby," Carol said, wanting to get out of the room. It was contaminated with fear.

As soon as she saw him in the lobby, Carol could tell from Ramsey's face that he had nothing good to report. He took them aside and told them: "We found no evidence that the girls were on the yacht. And we haven't found them on the island."

"Did you look for them at the Russians' house?" Brian asked.

"Inspector McGuire went there last evening. The Russians weren't there, but one of their women let him look around. He didn't see any sign of the girls."

"How many Russians are there?"

"Two. They say they're brothers, and they look alike. Their women are from here," Ramsey added as if he felt they were being exploited.

"Do they have permits to carry guns?"

"Oh, yes. It was one of their conditions for investing here. They claimed they needed them for protection."

"Why does your government allow them to operate here?"

Ramsey paused only a moment before saying: "For the same

reason that your government allows them to operate in your country."

"You mean Russians?"

"I mean criminal organizations."

"I'm sorry," Brian said. "I didn't mean to sound—"

"I understand. You want to blame someone," Ramsey said, "and if I was in your position I would too. It's a parent's worst nightmare."

"What are you going to do now?" Carol asked.

"Well, even though we found no evidence that the girls were on the yacht, we're going to operate on the assumption that they *were* on it, and that they were transferred to another boat. And we're going to work with your government to find them."

"What about your government?" Brian asked. "They must know something."

"Our government's corrupt," Ramsey said, "but they're not involved in this kind of thing, so they wouldn't have any useful information."

"Yet they take money from criminals."

"All politicians take money from criminals."

"Okay," Carol said, not caring about the politics. "You're going to work with our government to find the girls. How can we help you?"

"You can help," Ramsey said, "by calling the parents of your daughter's friend. I'll talk with them, but I think you should talk with them first."

"They'll want to come here," Brian said.

"Of course they will," Ramsey said.

"I don't want to leave the island," Carol said, "until we find out what happened."

"That could take a while. And as parents you have other responsibilities."

She didn't need to be reminded that they had a son who was coming home on Sunday, and that he expected them to be there waiting for him. That gave them only three more days to find out what happened, and Carol felt that if they left the island before they did find out, it would be as if they abandoned the girls.

When Ramsey had left they went into the dining room where the hotel served a buffet breakfast. From the many offerings, which turned her stomach, Carol selected a piece of toast without butter, and she made herself a cup of green tea. Brian got a bowl of plain yogurt with walnuts and honey. At this early hour they were the only guests in the dining room, so they could sit anywhere, and they went to a table in the corner.

"I'll talk with Donna," Carol said, breaking her toast.

"No, I'll talk with Richard."

"I'm the one who invited Stacy."

"We both invited her," Brian said, suspending the motion that would have carried a spoonful to his mouth. "Whatever happens, we're in this together."

"Thanks," she said, reaching for his other hand. "But I still want to talk with Donna."

"Then I'll talk with Richard after you talk with her."

Carol took a small bite of toast, and chewing, she said: "I hate to tell her over the phone, but there's no other way."

"They might not understand why we waited so long to tell them, but we really didn't know anything until this morning."

"We still don't know anything."

"I guess we don't. We only have a theory."

"Well, I wonder if the police know what they're doing."

"I thought you had confidence in the police," Brian said with a look of surprise.

"I do have confidence in them," she said. "But at the same time I'm looking for a reason why they could be wrong."

"They could be wrong for a lot of reasons. But they have some facts to support their theory. They have the damaged phone, and they have the fact that the yacht left the island around the time when the girls went missing. They also have the fact that every year a few girls go missing."

"The inspector said that. Did he say it started happening after the Russians came here?"

"I don't think he did, but I think he implied it."

"Okay. They have some facts to support their theory. But they didn't find any evidence that the girls were on the yacht."

"They didn't. But that doesn't prove the girls weren't on it."

Carol swallowed, and to wash down the toast she drank some tea. "Then we have to accept their theory?"

"No. But we have to go along with it until we find a reason why they could be wrong."

"So we're still hoping they could be wrong?"

"I don't see what else we can do," Brian said, lifting her hand and pressing it to the side of his face. "Except pray."

As they walked by the desk the man behind it told them the manager would like to see them. He led them back into an office where a man in a fawn-colored suit greeted them and expressed his concern about the girls, though while he talked in a polished accent he wasn't able to hide his concern about how the incident might affect the hotel. He told them that if they needed anything they should contact him directly.

They left his office with his business card, and they were back in their room by seven thirty. The island was normally an hour ahead of New York, but with daylight savings they were on the same time, so they had to call the Walkers now before they left for work.

Seated in one of the chairs while Brian paced the floor in front of her, Carol used her cell phone to make the call so that Donna would see who was calling and would answer instead of having her leave a message.

"Hi, Carol," Donna said brightly.

"Hi," Carol said, holding back.

"I hope the girls aren't driving you crazy."

"No, they're not. As a matter of fact—"

"I really appreciate your taking Stacy with you."

"—the girls are missing."

35

There was a long empty silence. "What do you mean?"

"I mean we don't know where they are. They left the resort."

"You don't know where they are?" Donna said in a voice that was rising to a level of hysteria. "How could you not know where they are?"

"The police are looking for them, but so far they haven't been able to find them."

"The police haven't been able to find them?" By now Donna was shrieking, and there was a sound of a resonant male voice in the background.

"Carol?" It was Richard. "What's going on?"

"The girls are missing."

"What do you mean?"

"They left the resort, and—"

"How the hell did leave the resort?"

"They walked out. The gate isn't locked."

"You weren't watching them?"

"They were playing tennis, and we took our eyes off them for a while. And for some reason they left the resort."

"When did this happen?"

"Yesterday, around three thirty."

"And you waited until *now* to tell us about it?"

"We didn't know what happened to them," Carol said, "and we still don't know."

"I want to talk with Brian," Richard said as if it was no use talking with her.

By then Brian had stopped in front of her, ready to help her, and she handed him the phone.

"Richard?" he said, bracing himself.

From then on she could hear only Brian's side of the conversation. "The police are looking for them...No. They're local. It's an independent country...I believe they are...They're working with our government...There's no American embassy here. There's an embassy in Barbados...Okay...Okay. Just let us know when your flight will arrive. We'll meet you at the airport."

He ended the call and handed back her phone.

"I didn't think it was possible to feel worse," she told him, "but when I heard Donna—"

"I know," he said. "I could hear her in the background."

"I guess I'd react the same way if someone called us on the phone and told us our daughter was missing."

"I don't think you would. At least you wouldn't become hysterical."

"I'm on the edge of hysteria. And if I believed the police's theory, I'd be over the edge."

"I didn't want to go into that over the phone," Brian said.

"I gather he asked you about the police."

"He asked if they were British, meaning white. And when I told him they were local, he asked if I thought they were competent. I told him I believe they are."

"I believe they are," Carol said.

"He said we should go to the American embassy—as if that was the solution. I told him there wasn't an embassy here. And he said he'd contact the embassy in Barbados, though they must already know about it."

"Why would they know about it?"

"The police are working with our government."

"Oh, yeah. Did he say anything else?"

"No. Except that they'll be here as soon as possible."

"Well, they won't make the flight we took," Carol said, remembering how hard it had been to pry the girls out of bed at five thirty in the morning in order to make the flight to Antigua. They had fallen back asleep on the way to the airport. "As I remember the schedules, that was the only non-stop flight to Antigua, so they might not get here until tomorrow."

"I hope they don't," Brian said, expressing her sentiment. "By then maybe we'll know more."

As she sat there holding her phone she felt the heavy weight of fatigue, having gotten no sleep the night before, and it took an effort for her to raise herself from the chair and walk to the bed and lie down. She set her phone on the table next to the bed, where she could easily reach it, and lying on her back, she closed her eyes and prayed: "Oh, please let them be found on the island, safe and sound."

At that moment she felt her husband next to her, and she rolled over and buried her face against his chest and cried her heart out.

They managed to sleep for a while, but they were awakened abruptly by the hotel phone. She fumbled the receiver, and then recovered it. "Hello?"

"Mrs. Delaney?" It was the deskman. "A television reporter is here to see you."

"A television reporter?" She hadn't realized that the island had a television station.

"If you don't want to, you don't have to talk with him."

"Well, please ask him to wait a minute," Carol said. "I'll call you right back."

She hung up and told Brian who it was.

"He must have found out about it from the police," Brian said. "I don't feel like talking with him, but maybe it would be helpful."

"How would it be helpful?"

"It would get the story out to the media, and we'd have more people looking for the girls."

"But I don't want to do anything that would interfere with the police."

"Then let's ask Ramsey what we should do."

She called Ramsey, using her phone.

After three rings Ramsey answered, and she explained the situation to him. "We don't feel like talking with him, but we can see how it would be helpful."

"I don't usually like to get the media involved," Ramsey told her, "but in this situation I think it would be helpful. The more people we have looking for the girls, the better chance we have of finding them."

"Okay. We'll talk with him. Is there anything we shouldn't tell him?"

"Don't tell him about your daughter's phone, and don't tell him we found no evidence that the girls were on the yacht."

"Can we tell him about your theory?"

"You can. Since we searched their yacht, the Russians already know about it. They just don't know what evidence we might have on them."

After ending the call she reported the conversation to Brian.

While talking with the detective she had become aware of the odor emanating from her underarms as a result of her nervous sweat, so she told the deskman they would see the reporter in about ten minutes, which gave her time to take a quick shower. This time she went first, and Brian went after her.

They were barely dressed when there was a discreet knock on the door.

Brian opened it, revealing a man with sun-bleached hair and the well-developed shoulders of a swimmer, equipped with a notebook and a camera.

"I'm Keith Hamilton from ZBF-TV," he said, showing his identification. He had an English accent but he didn't talk like the people on the BBC News. "I'm sorry about your situation, and I appreciate your being willing to talk with me."

"Come in," Brian said, stepping back.

Keith advanced into the room, and Carol invited him to sit down at the table.

"I cover the police beat for the station," Keith told them.

"Is there a lot of crime here?" Brian asked.

"More than they let on. But most of it happens to people who live here, so the outside world doesn't know about it."

"We heard this isn't the first time girls have gone missing."

"It isn't, but it's the first time since I've been here that *white* girls have gone missing."

"How long have you been here?"

"Eleven years," Keith said as if he couldn't believe it. He opened his notebook. "If you don't mind, I'd like to get some basic facts about you."

"We don't mind," Carol said.

"Well, I know your last name is Delaney, but what are your first names?"

"Carol and Brian."

"Where are you from?"

"We're from Hastings-on-Hudson. It's a village on the river about twenty miles north of New York City."

"It sounds like an English town."

"I guess it's supposed to."

Keith smiled, revealing teeth that hadn't been very well maintained. "And what are your professions?"

"My husband's an architect, and I'm a fund raiser."

"Do you work for one of those big firms?" Keith asked Brian.

"No. I'm self-employed. I have an office in our village."

"What about you?" Keith asked Carol.

"I work for a college in Yonkers."

"Yonkers, New York?"

"That's right."

Keith made a note. "So you're here on vacation with your daughter and her friend. What are their names?"

"Amanda and Stacy."

"How old are they?"

"Twelve."

"They're kids."

"Yeah."

"Do you think they could be pulling a prank?"

"They could be. I hope they are."

"When I was their age I did things that worried my mum."

"I'm sure she forgave you."

"She always did. Now, which of these girls is your daughter?"

"Amanda. Stacy's her friend."

"Could you give me the names of Stacy's parents?"

Carol hesitated, looking at Brian.

"I don't know why not," he said, reminding her with a facial expression that there were only two things the detective had asked them not to tell the reporter.

"Richard and Donna Walker," she told him. "They live in Hastings too."

"Could you tell me their professions?"

"He's a lawyer, and she's a graphic designer."

"Where are they now?"

"They're on their way here."

"They are? Ah—" Keith looked as if he was imagining an extension of the story. "When did the girls go missing?"

"Yesterday afternoon. They left the resort on their own. They walked into town, they bought ice cream cones, and they walked to the harbor."

Keith waited for her to tell him more.

"That's it. They didn't come back from the harbor."

"When did you decide to call the police?"

"When we couldn't find them."

"What time was that?"

"Around five," Brian said.

"I heard that a certain yacht went out around the time when the girls went missing. Do you think there's a connection?"

"We don't know what to think."

"I heard that the police searched the yacht."

"They did search it, but they didn't tell us what they found."

"It sounds like the police believe that the yacht took the girls off the island."

"We don't know. We hope the girls are still here."

"I hope they are too," Keith said as if he didn't relish the alternative. He reviewed his notes, and then he asked: "Is there anything else you want to say?"

"There is," Carol said, leaning forward. "I want to ask your viewers to report anything they might have seen that could help the police find the girls."

"I would have had you do that anyway," Keith said, closing his notebook. "So let me get some footage of you appealing to our viewers."

Keith got some footage of them together and some of Carol

making her appeal, and then he said: "I could use a picture of the girls."

"I have one on my phone."

"Will you send it to me?"

"I'll do it right now. What's your number?"

He gave it to her, and she sent the picture. Holding his phone, he waited for it, and when he saw it he said: "Lovely."

When the reporter had left they got up and walked to the beach and watched the children playing in the water. Carol remembered how within minutes of their arrival the girls had changed into their swimsuits and raced to the beach. She had gone right after them to make sure they would be safe, and she had watched them dance around in the waves in the sheer delight of being young and healthy and careless and free. And where were they now? Were they hiding in a cane field? Were they lying dead at the side of a road? Were they being held for ransom? Were they being transported to a slave market?

She reached for Brian's hand and held it, trying to withstand the terror that hit her like a giant breaker. Though she might have wanted to be crushed into oblivion and not have to think about the fate of the girls, she had to hold herself together, not only for her daughter but also for her son. Whatever had happened, she would have to deal with it.

At that moment her phone rang. It was Richard, who told her they hadn't been able to get a flight that arrived at St. Anselm today. They would have to sleep over at the Miami airport and catch a flight the next morning.

"So when will you arrive?"

"At four fifty. We'll be on a flight from Antigua."

"Okay. We'll meet you at the airport."

"I assume the police haven't found the girls."

"They haven't. We talked with the detective less than an hour ago, and he had nothing new to report. But they're still searching the island."

"We need to take over this operation," Richard said as if he was ready to send in the marines. "I put in a call to our embassy in Barbados. I haven't heard back from them, but when I do I'll light a fire under them."

"Before you make any judgments," Carol told him, "you should meet with the detective."

"I intend to. In fact, I want you to schedule a meeting with him at five thirty."

Though she felt she had just been treated like a secretary, she said: "Okay."

She reported the conversation to Brian, who said: "That's fine. I don't think I could deal with him today. He's acting like an ugly American."

"You mean he's assuming the police here are incompetent because they're not white?"

"That's what it sounds like, and that's what I heard when I talked with him before."

"You told him they're working with our government."

"Yeah. But that's not enough for him."

As they walked back to the hotel Carol remembered her father saying you don't know what people are really like until you're in a crisis with them. They had known the Walkers for years, or they had thought they knew them. Now, in a crisis, they would find out what the Walkers were really like.

With all that the resort offered, they could have passed the time swimming or playing tennis or eating or drinking, but they didn't feel like doing any of these things. In fact, they realized that a resort was probably the worst place to be while you were waiting to hear the fate of a missing child. And it felt like the day would never end.

Lying on the bed with Brian beside her, Carol gazed at the picture in her phone that she had given to the police and the reporter, trying to find in Amanda's eyes a clue about what had made her leave the resort, but all she saw was a look of innocent happiness. Amanda's eyes were the color of sunlit tropical water.

They went with her hair, which was nominally red but was actually orange. They had decided it came from Brian's side of the family since there were no redheads on Carol's side—her mother's family, who were from Naples, all had dark hair, and her father's family, who were from Sligo, all had brown hair. But there was red hair on Brian's side, including an aunt and a second cousin. Her flaming hair made Amanda stand out in a crowd, and it could have made her a target for the Russians. Maybe they wouldn't have noticed her if she'd had dark hair like her mother.

Carol set her phone on the bedside table and curled up as if she had been poisoned.

Around five Ramsey came to see them. They went to the snack bar and sat at the table where the two boys had been sitting the previous day.

"We've searched everywhere," Ramsey told them. "And we haven't found a trace of them. We're ready to conclude that they're not on the island."

"I had a thought while we were standing at the beach," Carol said. "Could someone have killed them and hidden the bodies?"

"When girls go missing, that's the first thought we have."

"You didn't mention that," Brian said.

"I didn't? I guess I was trying to spare you."

"So you've been looking for bodies?" Carol asked.

"We've been looking in all the usual places where killers hide bodies," Ramsey said. "So I think we can almost rule out the possibility that they were killed on the island."

"But they could have been killed somewhere else," Brian said.

"Yes. They could have been. But they're worth more alive to whoever took them."

For a moment, imagining why the girls might have value for whoever took them, she wasn't sure if she wanted them to be alive. But then her mother's instinct prevailed. "Well, I guess that's something we can hang on to."

"Have you heard from our government?" Brian asked.

"We get periodic reports from them. They've stopped a few

boats, but they haven't found a trace of the girls. They're still searching."

"Do you think it's possible that the boat they were on has already landed?"

"It's possible. The authorities in every port have their picture, but there are places along the coasts where boats can unload their cargos without being seen."

"What kind of cargos?"

"Drugs or humans."

"Is there a lot of human trafficking?"

"There's more than people imagine. My ancestors were brought to this island as slaves," Ramsey said. "They were brought in ships, stacked like cordwood. They spent their short lives cutting cane and doing other work that their masters weren't willing to do. Officially, slavery was abolished a long time ago. But it never stopped, and along with drugs, it's the biggest source of income for organized crime. And it's everywhere, it's a global business."

"If there's so much of it, why don't we stop it?"

"For the same reason that we don't stop drug trafficking."

Brian frowned. "You mean we don't want to stop it?"

"No, I mean *they* don't want to stop it."

"Who are they?"

"The people who make money from it. And that includes the governments," Ramsey added. "Even yours."

"But how can you say that?" Brian objected. "You're working with our government."

"I'm working with people in your government who are at my level. They're not the ones who make money from crime."

"Well, aren't there more people at your level than there are at a high level?"

"There are, but we don't have the power. Since I trust you," Ramsey said, leaning confidentially toward them, "I can tell you that the Russians complained about us searching their yacht, and we got an order from a high level not to interfere with them."

"Will you obey it?"

"I'll pretend to. Did Keith ask if you knew what we found on the yacht?"

"He didn't ask," Carol said. "But we said you didn't tell us what you found."

"That's good. He'll know how to use that."

"You want them to think you found something?"

"I do," Ramsey said softly. "And I want them to wonder what it was. I want them to go crazy wondering what it was."

FOUR

AT SIX THAT evening they watched the television story about the missing girls. The commentator, a pretty brown woman with perfectly styled black hair, recounted the facts they had given to Keith, and then she said: "The police continue to search the island, though they suspect that the girls were taken away by a yacht whose owners live on St. Anselm. They searched the yacht, but they won't disclose what they found on it."

Carol appreciated how carefully the last sentence had been written to imply that the police *had* found something on the yacht, and knowing that Ramsey had gotten an order from a high level not to interfere with the Russians, she marveled at how he had enlisted the cooperation of the television station, which she assumed was privately owned.

The story ended with the footage of Carol pleading with viewers to report anything they might have seen that could help the police find the girls.

When a male commentator began talking passionately about cricket, Brian shut off the television, and they decided to go and have some dinner, if for no other reason than to kill time since neither of them felt like eating.

On their way back to the room after dinner they stopped at the desk to reserve a room for the Walkers. The deskman told them he thought the hotel would able to accommodate them, but he couldn't guarantee anything until the next day.

They had another long night, though by now they were so fatigued that they were able to sleep intermittently. When one of them awoke, the other usually did too, but around three in the morning Carol awoke and Brian kept sleeping. While she envied his state of oblivion, she knew how he was hurting—Amanda

47

was his treasure—and she was thankful that he was being given some respite from the pain he would have felt if he were awake at this dark hour. And she lay still, not wanting to disturb him.

She imagined the girls in the cabin of a boat that was taking them to an unknown destination. They were probably being watched by a thug, who had a gun that he threatened to use at the slightest provocation. They had no idea what their captors planned to do with them since they didn't know that such things happened in the world.

Of course they had been warned by their parents not to talk with strangers, but until now they had never been in a situation where they were at risk of being molested. They walked to school through a safe neighborhood, and they were driven everywhere else by their parents. They never went anywhere on their own. For that reason Carol had told them not to leave the resort on their own, but she must not have impressed on them strongly enough that the world outside the gate was dangerous. And she blamed herself for bringing them here, for believing they would be perfectly safe inside the walls of the Royal Palms. She blamed herself for not watching them closely enough, for not guessing they were up to something when she let them play another set of tennis. She blamed herself for what she imagined was happening to them right now.

The next morning, when they stopped at the desk after breakfast, they were informed that the Walkers would have to stay in the girls' room since nothing else was available, so Carol went to straighten it up. The bed had been made and the bathroom had been cleaned by the hotel staff, but clothes were strewn around, the tennis rackets were on the chair, and Bo was sitting on the desk where she had left him. She gathered the clothes and hung some in the closet and put some in drawers, tenderly folding a top she had bought for Amanda the weekend before they left on vacation. Amanda had worn it to dinner their first night here, and with a sudden pang of fear Carol wondered if her daughter would ever have a chance to wear it again.

When she was done she left the room and brought Bo with her, holding him tightly against her chest and smelling Amanda in his tee-shirt.

At quarter after four they verified that the flight from Antigua was on time and they got a taxi and went to the airport. They waited for the Walkers in the area where arriving passengers emerged from immigration and customs. The only other person waiting was a jittery man with a sign that said "Bachman."

Finally appearing, Richard and Donna looked as if they had no idea where they were.

Carol waved at them to get their attention.

Donna rushed to her, crying: "Oh, please tell me the police have found them."

"I'm sorry," Carol told her. "They're still missing."

Donna broke down, and Carol held her, wishing there was something she could say to comfort her friend.

"I heard from the embassy," Richard said, a few steps behind his wife. "They told me our ships are looking for the girls."

"That's good," Brian said as if he hadn't known this.

Richard had a bag slung over his shoulder like a weapon. He and Brian played tennis twice a week, even in the winter under the bubble that the club inflated over the courts, and Richard could tell you at any time who was ahead in the competition. "But they don't know what kind of boat they're looking for, so they need more information."

"I'm sure the police gave them all the information they had," Brian said.

"Then they need to get more information."

"We have a meeting with the police at five thirty. Maybe they'll know more by then."

"If they don't," Richard said, "then we'll have to kick ass."

They walked over to the baggage area, where there was no activity yet.

Donna was still crying, and Carol kept an arm around her waist.

"You know, when I called the hotel yesterday to reserve a room," Richard said caustically, "they told me they were full."

"They put you in the girls' room," Brian said.

"They finally did. But imagine telling me they were full."

"Did they know who you were?"

"I gave them my name," Richard said. "They should have made the connection. I had to make it for them, and I had to tell them that if they didn't find a room for us they'd face an even bigger lawsuit."

It sounded like Richard was building a case against the people on the island, and Carol didn't like where she thought he was going, but she let her husband handle him since she had her hands full with Donna.

When the baggage arrived Richard retrieved two small suitcases that could have been carried on to a larger plane, and they headed for the taxi.

"Are we going to the hotel first?" Richard asked.

"I think it would be better," Brian said. "We have enough time to go there first."

The driver, a mellow old gentleman, opened the trunk of his car and helped Richard put in the suitcases. He also offered to take the bag that was slung over Richards's shoulder, but Richard wouldn't let him touch it.

Since there wasn't room for all of them in the back seat, Brian sat in front.

As they rolled out of the parking lot Richard said: "I don't think we should all meet with the police. I think only Brian and I should meet with them."

"I want to meet with them," Donna said, drying her eyes with the back of her hand.

"I think we should all meet with them," Brian said.

"Okay," Richard said, "but with so many people it'll be less efficient."

"But it might be more effective," Carol said.

They rode in silence the rest of the way. It was obvious that

Richard had a lot more to say but didn't want to say it in front of the driver.

They arrived at the hotel, and Richard checked in, already complaining about the service.

"We'll wait for you here," Brian told him as the porter took their luggage toward the elevator.

"Okay. We'll be right back," Richard said. "And then we'll go and raise hell with the police."

As soon as the elevator door had closed, Carol said: "I don't like Richard's behavior."

"I don't either," Brian said, "but I understand it. He thinks the police haven't done enough to find the girls, and he's here to make sure they do their job."

"Well, I hope he doesn't offend Ramsey."

"I think Ramsey can handle him."

When the Walkers returned to the lobby they all went out and got into the taxi, which they had asked to wait for them. This time Richard sat in front.

"I had no idea this island was so poor," Donna said, looking out the window at the shanties as they followed the potholed road into town.

"The only source of income is tourism," Richard said, an instant expert on St. Anselm. "And the only jobs are at the resorts."

From what she had seen Carol didn't think it was quite that simple but she didn't comment.

They were greeted at the police station by Inspector McGuire, who after introducing himself to the Walkers led them back to Ramsey's office.

"Please sit down," Ramsey said after shaking hands.

"You probably know I'm a lawyer," Richard began. "I'm not a criminal lawyer, but I know something about police procedures. So I want you to tell me what you've done from the time you received the call from Brian."

"Actually," McGuire said, "we got the call from Derek, a security guard at the Royal Palms."

"Inspector McGuire will give you his side of it," Ramsey said, "and then I'll give you mine."

After hearing the whole story, which he interrupted from time to time to ask a question, Richard said: "I talked with a man in our consular section in Barbados, and he told me our ships don't know what kind of boat they're looking for, so they need more information."

"We told them everything we knew. But since you mentioned it," Ramsey said, exchanging a look with McGuire. "There *is* a way to get more information, but we need the cooperation of your government."

"What do you want them to do?" Richard asked.

"We want them to monitor the Russian yacht."

"But wouldn't that be a waste of time? The girls aren't on it."

Ramsey leaned forward, tenting his hands. "We believe the Russians are involved in criminal activities. If your government catches them at something else, we might be able to get them to tell us where they took the girls."

"Are they residents of your country?"

"Yes. They're special residents."

"What does that mean?"

"It means we can't arrest them," McGuire said, "unless we catch them in the act of committing a crime."

"Then you should ask our government to monitor the yacht."

"I think it would be better if you asked them," Ramsey said. "They're your government, and you have a relationship with your embassy in Barbados."

"I'll call them right now," Richard said, taking out his phone. He made a call, but the man he had talked to wasn't available so he left a message. Frustrated, he said: "I don't see why you need to catch those guys at something else. You know they took the girls."

"We believe they did, but we can't prove it."

"What about the cell phone? You should have found their fingerprints on it."

"We checked for prints," Ramsey said patiently, "but there

wasn't anything useful. Several people handled the phone after they found it."

"They shouldn't have handled it."

"They didn't know it was evidence."

Carol appreciated Ramsey's defense of their actions at the harbor. Still, she regretted handling the phone and smudging the fingerprints of the man who had grabbed it from Amanda.

"Well, you must have something else on them."

"Unfortunately, we don't," Ramsey said. "And we can't torture them to make them talk."

"I'll make those bastards talk," Richard blustered. "Tell me where they live."

"If I were you," McGuire said, "I wouldn't go there."

"Why not? If they hurt me, you'd have something on them?"

"No, we wouldn't. They'd claim they caught you trying to break into their house."

"Are you sure the girls aren't on the island?" Donna asked hopefully.

"We're not a hundred percent sure, but almost."

"Did another boat leave the island around the time when the girls went missing?" Richard asked.

"We asked at all the harbors," Ramsey told him, "and no one saw a boat leave the island around that time."

"The fishing boats come in at that time," McGuire said.

"What about a plane?" Richard asked.

"There's only one airport," Ramsey said, "and no plane left around that time."

"Then you *know* the Russians took them."

"We still can't prove it. That's why it would be helpful to catch them at something else."

At that moment Richard's phone rang. It was the embassy, and Carol could hear only one side of the conversation. "I'm with the St. Anselm police now...They want you to monitor the Russian yacht...What's its name?"

"*Pikovaya Dama,*" McGuire said.

Richard repeated the name, and after listening for a while he said: "He wants to know what evidence you have that the girls were on the yacht."

"Two fishermen saw it leave the harbor around the time when the girls went missing."

Richard relayed that, and then he asked: "Can you fax them a statement from the fishermen?"

"Sure. He wants to cover his ass," Ramsey muttered.

"What's his fax number?" McGuire asked.

Richard got it and gave it to McGuire, who left the room to have the fax sent. He said into his phone: "It's on the way."

When the call had ended, Brian asked: "Is the yacht in the harbor?"

"Yes," Ramsey said. "We have a man watching it."

"But if it's in the harbor, you won't catch it doing anything."

"You're right. We won't. So we'll have to wait until the yacht goes out to sea."

"I don't think I can stand waiting," Donna said, beginning to break down again. "I want to know what happened to my child."

"I can imagine how you feel," Ramsey said gently. "I have two girls, and I worry about them."

"But you're a policeman. You can protect them."

"No, I can't. And if they went missing, I couldn't do more than I'm doing now."

McGuire returned and told them the fax had been sent to the embassy. Since at that moment even Richard didn't have any more ideas, they ended the meeting.

Back at the hotel they went to the snack bar and sat at the table in the corner to assess the situation. The men ordered coffees, and the women ordered seltzers. Other than the boys who were playing tennis next to the girls before they went missing, there was no one else at the snack bar since for most people it was probably time for dinner.

"I think the Russians are the key to it," Richard said as if he had made a discovery.

54

"I think they are," Brian said. "And so do the police."

"Well, what do we know about them?"

"We only know what the police told us. They came to the island with a lot of money, they built a big house, and they have business operations."

"What kind of business operations?"

"The police believe they're involved in criminal activities. But they can't prove it."

"Maybe they don't want to prove it."

"What are you suggesting?"

"I'm suggesting the police are on the take, as they are in all these countries."

"I don't think they are," Carol said, disagreeing strongly.

"That's your opinion," Richard said.

"It's more than an opinion. It's a feeling."

"A feeling," Richard snorted. "Then why don't they go after the Russians more aggressively?"

"They got our ships to stop the yacht," Brian said. "And they searched the yacht when it came back to the harbor. If they were on the take, they wouldn't have done those things."

"They could have only gone through the motions," Richard argued. "They could have warned the Russians that our ships were after them. And they could have destroyed any evidence they found when they searched the yacht."

"The Russians complained about the police searching their yacht," Brian said, "and the police got an order from a high level not to interfere with them."

"That's what the police told you."

"I believe them," Carol said.

"Well, I don't think they know what they're doing," Richard said. "I think our government should take over."

"They've already taken over the search," Brian said.

"They should take over the whole investigation."

"Because you don't trust the island police?"

"That's right. I don't trust them."

"Are you biased?" Carol asked.

"No, I'm not biased," Richard said.

"Well, I heard you make a generalization about the police in these countries. You said they're all on the take."

"They are. They don't get paid enough, so they have to make money on the side."

"Maybe some of them do, but I don't believe McGuire and Ramsey make money on the side."

"You don't know them," Richard said. "You have no idea what they do when you're not looking."

"This isn't getting us anywhere," Brian said.

"Okay," Richard admitted. "But I still think our government should take over, and unless someone has a better idea—"

"I have a better idea," Carol said. "I think we should offer a reward for information that helps us find the girls."

"That's not such a bad idea," Richard conceded. "How much should we offer?"

"A million dollars," Carol said without hesitation.

"We don't have that kind of money."

"We could get it. We could borrow on our homes, we could cash in our pension plans—"

"We'd find a way to get the money," Brian said, supporting her.

For the first time since he had arrived on the island Richard was silenced.

"They're right," Donna said, finally entering the conversation. "I don't care what we have to do. I want to find our daughter."

"Okay," Richard said. "I'll go along with you."

"So we're going to offer a million dollars," Carol said, "for information that helps us find the girls."

"For information that *enables* us to find them," Richard said, acting as a lawyer. "But I have a concern. If the girls are being held for ransom, wouldn't offering such a big reward encourage the kidnappers to ask for more?"

"It could," Brian said. "But they haven't asked for money."

"They might not be holding the girls for ransom," Carol said, feeling it was time to broach the subject.

56

"Why else would they be holding them?" Donna asked as if no one had told her.

"They might be holding them for commercial purposes," Brian said, stopping short of saying it.

"What do you mean?"

"He means," Richard said bluntly, "that the men who took them might be involved in human trafficking."

"Oh, my God," Donna cried, clapping her hand to her mouth as if to prevent herself from throwing up. She glared at her husband. "And you're worried about having to pay more to get our daughter back?"

"I was only voicing a concern," Richard told her.

"You mean a concern about money."

"No. I don't care how much we have to pay to get her back."

"Then let's put the word out," Brian said.

They made the phone calls from the table. Brian called Ramsey and the reporter, and Richard called the embassy. Brian settled the bill with the waiter, and they went to their rooms without mentioning the possibility of having dinner together.

Around nine they ordered a grilled chicken sandwich from room service, which they split and ate at the table. And then, out of curiosity, Brian turned on the television and got the local news in time to hear the weather.

After the five-day forecast an anchorwoman reported a new development in the story about the missing girls. Sitting in front of a panoramic view of the island, she announced: "We have just learned that the parents are offering a reward of one million U.S. dollars for information that enables them to find their daughters. This is a picture that was taken of the girls shortly before they went missing."

The screen showed Amanda and Stacy in their tennis clothes.

"If you've seen them, or if you have any information on their whereabouts, please call the number on your screen."

"That was fast," Brian said.

"Yeah, I'm impressed," Carol said, feeling a little better about their chances of finding the girls.

When they went to bed she held Bo between her and Brian, still smelling Amanda in the bear's tee-shirt but knowing that eventually even that comfort would wear off.

When they went to the dining room for breakfast the next morning they saw Richard sitting at a table alone, and they joined him after going through the buffet.

"Is Donna all right?" Carol asked.

"She's not doing well," Richard said.

"Do you think it might help if I talked with her?"

"It might, but not now. When I left her a few minutes ago she'd finally gone to sleep."

"It's hard to sleep. You keep thinking—" She didn't have to finish the sentence.

"The word about our reward went out," Brian told Richard after a pause. "They announced it last night on the local news."

"I hope it goes beyond this island," Richard said.

"It will. I'm sure the wire services will pick up the story."

"I still think the police could get more information from the Russians if they wanted to."

"They want to, but their hands are tied."

"Then our government should tell their government to let the police do their job."

"I'm sure our government will talk with theirs," Brian said calmly. "But we haven't been effective telling other governments what to do."

"This isn't Iraq or Afghanistan. It's a pissant island."

"Still, they have their pride."

"Well, their pride," Richard said, "shouldn't get in the way of a criminal investigation."

"It shouldn't, but it could. So let's hope our ambassador is a good diplomat."

On the way back to their rooms Carol asked Richard to let her know when Donna woke up so she could talk with her.

A half hour later Donna called her, and they agreed to meet in the corridor.

"I have to get out of that room," Donna told her. "I keep seeing Stacy's clothes."

"Let's take a walk. We can go to the beach."

When they were outside Carol took her friend's arm the way she took Amanda's arm when they crossed a street.

There were people lying around the pool as if they didn't have a care in the world.

"It was bad enough," Donna said, "imagining Stacy being held for ransom, but imagining her being trafficked for sex— I can't deal with it."

"I know. It's hard. It's the last thing I'd ever imagine."

"I've read about it happening to girls. But I never thought it could happen to my daughter."

"I never did either," Carol said. "I still don't want to believe it's happening."

"If they're found in time, it won't happen."

"That's what I'm hoping. I'm even hoping they're being held for ransom."

"I am too," Donna said. "I can't believe I am, but I am. I guess no matter what happens to your child, there's always something worse that can happen."

They walked in silence the rest of the way, and they stood at the beach and watched the children playing in the water.

"Were they having a good time?" Donna asked.

"They were having a great time. They had everything here that they could want."

"Then why did they leave the resort?"

"I don't know. They might have wanted an adventure."

"But you told them not to leave on their own." It was neither a statement nor a question.

"We told them very clearly not to leave the resort on their own. But you know how it is," Carol said. "If you tell them not to do something, then they want to do it."

"I have to admit," Donna said, "my first thought was to blame you for not watching them."

"We did take our eyes off them for a while."

"But you couldn't watch them every second. I mean, they could have left the resort while you were sleeping."

"I don't think they would have at night."

"But you might have wanted to take a nap in the afternoon."

"We did take a nap," Carol said, stopping short of admitting they had made love. "But we took our eyes off them for only a half hour."

"If you'd taken your eyes off them for only five minutes, they could have slipped away. So I don't blame you."

"I blame myself."

"I know how you feel," Donna said. "Whenever anything bad happens to one of my children, I blame myself. But I want you to know I don't blame you."

"Thanks. That helps."

"I'm not only hoping the girls are found in time, but I'm also praying they're found in time. I haven't prayed in years, but I'm praying now."

"I'm praying too, but whatever faith I have is being tested. I mean, how could a loving God allow this kind of thing to happen?"

"I have the same question. So I guess I'm only praying on the chance that there *is* a God who won't let it happen."

"That's where I am. But I don't know where I'll be if He does let it happen."

With their arms around each other's waists, they gazed out at the endless ocean. Somewhere out there Amanda and Stacy were being taken away in a boat, captive. And whatever the purpose, time wasn't on their side.

That afternoon Ramsey came to the hotel and asked to talk with them. Again, they met at the snack bar and sat at the table in the corner.

Carol could tell from Ramsey's face that he didn't have good news for them.

"Your government contacted our government," he began.

"That's good," Richard said, interrupting.

"No," Ramsey said. "It's not good. They were making sure that our government wants them to monitor the yacht. And our government asked them not to."

"They did?" Richard said with indignation. "Why?"

"They treat the Russians as political refugees."

"Political refugees? From what?"

"From the persecution they suffered in their home country. They claim they came to our country for asylum, and now we're persecuting them."

"That's a load of crap."

"I know," Ramsey said. "But our government pretends to believe it. They like the money the Russians give them."

"Do they ask where the money comes from?"

"They don't care. Like most people who are offered money, they don't care where it comes from."

Richard glowered. "Well, the yacht is important to the case."

"I know. But our government told your government that it has nothing to do with the case."

"You have the fishermen's statement," Richard said as if the detective needed this reminder.

Ramsey sighed. "They retracted their statement. They said the police coerced them into making it."

"Why did they retract it?"

"They must have been threatened. They have children."

"They should have stood by their statement."

"They should have," Ramsey agreed, "but I understand why they didn't. So now we have no basis for asking your government to monitor the yacht."

"Is our government still searching for the girls?" Carol asked.

"Of course they are," Ramsey assured her. "They're stopping every boat, they're checking every harbor, they're following every lead, they're doing everything possible."

"They could be doing more," Richard said.

"What more could they be doing?" Ramsey asked.

"I don't know. I just think they could be doing more."

"What about the media?" Carol asked.

"The story's everywhere—television, radio, newspapers. And everyone knows about the reward," Ramsey added.

"Are you sure the girls aren't on the island?" Donna asked as if it was her last hope.

"By now I'm a hundred percent sure."

"So is there any reason for us to stay here?" Richard asked.

"No. You should go home. You have other children to worry about. But I want you to know," Ramsey said with determination, "I'm going to catch those gorillas at something, and when I do they're going to tell me where they took your daughters."

They all stood up and shook hands with Ramsey, and Carol thanked him.

When Ramsey had left them Brian called the airline and found a flight the next morning that would get them to New York in the early evening. He shared this information with the Walkers, and within a half hour they were all booked on that flight.

As they headed back to their room Carol said: "I feel like I'm leaving Amanda here."

"You're not," Brian said, putting an arm around her shoulder. "She's not here."

FIVE

WHILE THEY WAITED for their luggage at the airport Carol called the home of the friend who had taken Matthew skiing. She told Nancy, the friend's mother, that they had decided to return a day early, and that they were at the airport.

Nancy, who had a laid-back disposition that Carol sometimes envied, didn't ask why they had returned early. She welcomed Carol home and told her there was no rush since the boys were engrossed in a computer game.

Imagining how Matthew would be affected by the news of his sister's disappearance, Carol was glad he could enjoy another hour of carefree play.

They shared the airport car service with the Walkers, who were dropped off first since they lived on the hill, and while Brian gave the driver an extra tip she opened the front door of their house, which as usual stuck in the damp weather. The house was a hundred and seventy years old, and this was the original door. It was one of those things she had minded about living in an old house, but it seemed insignificant now.

As soon as they had carried in the suitcases Brian left to pick up Matthew, and Carol tried to prepare herself for a difficult conversation. On the plane they had discussed what they would say to Matthew, agreeing on the principles of telling him everything they knew and giving him hope that Amanda would be found and returned to them. She would have liked to tell Matthew there was nothing to worry about, but that wasn't true, and if she tried to pretend it was, her son would detect that it wasn't true, just as by the age of five he had detected that there wasn't a Santa Claus or an Easter Bunny.

63

She went into the kitchen, and to occupy the time she looked at the mail that the girl who watched their house while they were away had set on the table. It was mostly catalogs and bills, including a bill from Amanda's orthodontist. She was filled with outrage at the thought of a kid with braces being used for the purpose she feared.

"We're home," Brian said as he always did on returning with their children. It was more than a statement, it was a celebration that they were together.

"I'm in the kitchen," Carol called out.

She met them halfway, in the dining room, and she hugged Matthew thankfully, inhaling the smell of his unwashed hair and saying: "I missed you."

"I missed you too, mom," he said dutifully.

She stepped back and gazed at him. With his dark hair and dark eyes he took after her mother, the Italian side of the family. In fact, he looked like her brother and nothing at all like Brian. "Well, let's sit down and hear about your skiing trip."

They went into the kitchen, where they usually sat down together as a family.

"Would you like a soda?" Brian asked.

"No, thanks," Matthew said.

"Could you open some wine?" Carol asked, suddenly needing it. She took her usual chair near the stove, and Matthew took his usual chair opposite her.

"Is Amanda up in her room?" Matthew asked.

"She's not here," Carol told him, leading into it. "She didn't come home with us."

"She didn't?" Matthew said as if he suspected that his sister was getting a longer vacation. "Why didn't she?"

Carol reached out and took his hand, saying: "Amanda and Stacy are missing."

Matthew looked puzzled. "What do you mean?"

"I mean we don't know where they are."

"They were kidnapped," Brian said, uncorking a bottle.

64

"They were *kidnapped?*" Matthew said, unable to control his excitement. He looked as if he was experiencing what happened in the television programs he watched on his computer.

"While we weren't watching them," Carol said, continuing, "they left the resort."

"They left on their own?"

"Yeah. And they got into trouble."

"They walked to the harbor," Brian said, "where they were abducted and taken off the island."

"How were they taken off the island?"

"They were taken in a yacht."

"Then the police should be able to find them."

"They *will* find them," Carol said with as much faith as she could summon.

Brian brought the glass of wine to her and sat down opposite Amanda's empty chair.

"When did it happen?" Matthew asked as if he needed this information.

"On Monday," Brian said.

"Have you heard from the kidnappers?"

"No. We haven't," Carol said.

Evidently based on what he had learned from those television programs, Matthew said: "If it happened on Monday, you should have heard from them by now."

"The kidnappers might not be ready to call us," Brian said. "They might want to take the girls to a place where the police can't find them."

"You mean to a hideout?"

"Yeah, to a hideout."

Matthew was silent, and then he said: "If I'd gone with you, it wouldn't have happened."

So her son wouldn't blame himself for not going with them, Carol said: "We don't know what would have happened."

"Well, if I'd been with her, we wouldn't have left the resort on our own."

"You might have," Carol said. "You might have believed you

65

could protect her."

Matthew didn't dispute this. Instead, he asked: "Do you think the kidnappers will kill them?"

"I don't think they will," Brian said. "They have a reason to keep them alive."

"But don't kidnappers kill their hostages after they collect the ransom?"

"Sometimes they do. But I don't think we're dealing with that kind of kidnapper."

"What kind of kidnapper are we dealing with?"

"The kind who know they won't get caught."

Matthew paused to think about this. "So they won't have to eliminate witnesses?"

"That's right," Carol said with mixed feelings about his grasp of the situation.

"How much ransom will they want?"

"We have no idea. But whatever they want, we'll pay it. Don't worry."

This seemed to reassure Matthew, and Carol was glad that at least there was something she could tell him not to worry about.

Later, she went into Matthew's room and sat down on the edge of the bed, where he was lying on his back with the covers drawn up to his neck. She looked into his eyes and saw how he was hurting. He was past the age where he welcomed kisses from his mother, but tonight when she leaned over to kiss him he put his arms around her and held her tight. She asked: "Would you like to bring your sleeping bag into our room?"

"No. I'll be all right."

"I could give you Bo."

"No, thanks."

"Well, say a prayer for your sister."

"I will. I wonder where she is."

"She's somewhere in the Caribbean."

"Then maybe the pirates will rescue her."

"Maybe. I love you."

"I love you too."

When she and Brian finally went to bed she took Bo with her and held him as many years ago she had held the bear that comforted her in the scary hours of the night. Bo still smelled faintly of Amanda, which helped a little but wasn't enough to protect her from the nightmares of her imagination. With a cry of anguish she moved toward Brian, who put his arms around her and held her the same way she was holding their daughter's bear.

The next morning she went to Yonkers to see her parents, who didn't expect to see her until the next day, which was Palm Sunday. Her parents always had a traditional Italian feast on Palm Sunday, and her mother started the preparations the day before with a trip to Arthur Avenue in the Bronx to buy things she couldn't get at the supermarket.

Carol didn't want to deliver the bad news to her parents any sooner than necessary, but she couldn't show up for church the next day and explain why Amanda wasn't with them. On Palm Sunday and on Christmas they went with her parents to St. Denis, their church in the old neighborhood. The congregation had changed since they lived there, as reflected by the fact that the church had some masses in Spanish, but her parents knew people who still lived there and still went to St. Denis, so they remained loyal to that parish.

The house where they lived now was on Morningside Place. Her parents bought it during Carol's senior year of college, and a year later she moved to the city, so she didn't live there very long. She had grown up in an apartment on McLean Avenue near Radford Street, and she had been happy there. But her parents had always dreamed of owning a house up on the hill, and when they had finally saved enough money for a down payment they couldn't wait to leave the apartment. They also believed the neighborhood was changing for the worse.

Heading south on Broadway she passed Shonnard Place, then turned left on Lake Avenue and drove over to Morningside, where she turned left and looked for a parking place. The lots were narrow, and most of the houses didn't have driveways. Like the other houses on their side of the street her parents' house had a gable on the third floor, which was really an attic though it could be used for living space. It also had a small front porch, where on summer evenings her parents sat in plastic chairs.

She parked in front of a house that had recently been covered with light gray aluminum siding. Her parents' house had siding too, but it was yellow, her mother's favorite color. Her father had finally drawn the line when her mother wanted a yellow car—he said it would look like a taxi, and people would hail them, wanting a ride.

On the porch there were two chairs and a snow shovel. The chairs wouldn't have been used all winter since it hadn't been warm enough to sit outside, and the shovel wouldn't have been needed all winter since it hadn't snowed, except once in October. On the basis of that freak event her father had predicted a dire winter, repeating his view that all the talk about global warming was a lot of hooey, though he wouldn't have put it that way in the company of men.

She rang the bell as her father had taught her: a long, a short, a long, and a short, which was Morse code for the first letter of her name. Having warned her parents who it was, she walked in. It was only a few steps from the front door to the living room, and she saw her parents in the easy chairs they always sat in, watching television. Her father was holding a bottle of beer and her mother a glass of white wine.

"I thought you were coming back tomorrow," her mother said with a puzzled look.

"We were, but we changed our minds," Carol said, not yet ready to explain why.

"Well, I'm glad you're back. Did you have a good vacation?"

"Yeah. But it's good to be home."

"You don't look like you got any sun," her mother said, examining her face.

"She's Irish," her father said. "She doesn't get dark like Italians do."

"I'm half Italian," Carol said, welcoming the digression.

"No, you're not. You're all Irish, and your brother's all Italian. Your sister's half and half."

"She has a new boyfriend," her mother announced.

"That's good," Carol said. Her sister Paula, who lived in San Francisco, was thirty four and still single, changing boyfriends as often as she changed employers. She was now cooking in an "authentic" Mexican restaurant in the South of Market area.

"Would you like a beer?" her father asked.

"No, thanks. I'll get some wine."

"It's in the door of the refrigerator," her mother told her.

Carol went into the kitchen, where a pot of sauce was slowly cooking. There were other signs of the feast her mother was preparing for the next day, including jars of red peppers, artichoke hearts, and black olives. A thick sopresata was lying on the counter, with paper wrapped around its middle, and a box of rigatoni stood on the table.

She poured herself a glass of wine and lingered in the kitchen. Her parents had retired after working all their lives, her father as a mail carrier and her mother as a postal clerk. They had made a lot of sacrifices for their children, not renewing furniture or dining out or taking vacations so their children could go to Catholic schools and then go to college well prepared. Like other students at St. Catherine, Carol was the first in her family to go to college, and her parents celebrated her acceptance there by taking them all out to dinner at Spiritoso on McLean Avenue. Her brother Martin followed her at St. Catherine, and finally Paula, who stopped after two years and transferred to a cooking school. They all had jobs while going to college, helping to pay for it, but their parents underwrote the expense. So now that they were all supporting themselves, their parents deserved to enjoy life.

She knew how much it would upset her parents when she told them what had happened to Amanda, but knowing it would upset them more if they heard about the kidnapping first from the television, she went back into the living room and faced them.

"Mom, dad," she said, standing in front of them like a child in trouble, "something really terrible happened. Amanda and her friend were kidnapped."

"What?" they said, almost together.

"They were taken from the island, we think in a yacht."

"Now, wait a minute," her father said in anger. "What the hell are you talking about?"

"I'm talking about what happened to my daughter, your granddaughter. She and her friend were taken from the island."

"Who took them?" her father demanded.

"We don't know. The police believe it was some Russians."

"Russians? What are they doing in the Caribbean?"

"They live on the island."

"Then why haven't the police arrested them?"

"They can't prove it was the Russians. But they're working with our government, which has ships in the Caribbean, and they're searching everywhere."

After a silence her mother said: "I don't understand how someone could get into the resort and kidnap two girls."

"That's not how it happened," Carol said. "The girls left the resort on their own."

"They left the resort on their own?"

"Yeah. They were playing tennis, and we took our eyes off them for a moment."

"A moment?" her mother asked skeptically.

"Well, a half hour," Carol admitted, feeling the skewer of her mother's judgment. "I don't know what got into them. Amanda never did anything like that before."

"She probably never had the opportunity."

"What do you mean?"

"When you were her age," her mother said, "we didn't schedule your activities and chauffer you around. We let you play in the neighborhood with other kids."

"You mean I sheltered her too much?"

"I mean kids are being raised differently these days."

"Okay," her father said as if they had gotten her mother's

point. "Now, when were the girls taken from the island?"

"On Monday afternoon."

Her father deliberately counted on the fingers of the hand that wasn't holding the beer bottle. "That was five days ago. And you haven't heard from the kidnappers?"

"No." She didn't want to upset her parents even more by telling them the girls might have been trafficked, so she said: "The police say we should hear from them soon."

"What police?"

"The island police."

"So what are they doing?"

"They're doing everything possible to find the girls."

"I mean specifically."

"They're working with our government, with our embassy in Barbados, with our ships in the Caribbean, and with the police in all the ports where the girls could be taken. And just so you know what we're doing," Carol told them, "we and the parents of the other girl are offering a reward for information that enables us to find the girls."

"How much are you offering?"

"A million dollars."

"Really?" Her father was impressed. "Well, I know you don't have that kind of money, so we'll help you."

"Thanks, but we'll manage." The last thing she wanted was for her parents to make another sacrifice. They were able to get by on their pensions, but they had no money to spare.

"How's Matthew doing?" her mother asked.

"I don't know. I don't think it's really hit him yet."

"It's the last thing I ever would have expected to happen."

"Well, it did happen," Carol said, beginning to cry. "And I can't bear imagining my poor baby in the hands of those brutes."

With a look of sympathy her mother said: "She'll be all right. God will take care of her."

Carol didn't say what she felt like saying. She didn't want to give her mother one more thing to worry about.

The next day they went to church with her parents. They went to the mass in English, and Carol recognized some people from the old neighborhood, but they were outnumbered by the younger families who had moved into the affordable housing of South Yonkers. She felt a moment of joy at the sight of a Latino couple with two little girls who were all dressed up and holding palms in celebration of Christ's triumphal entry into Jerusalem.

After Communion she knelt and prayed for the safe return of Amanda and Stacy, but she didn't have much faith that God was listening. If He truly cared about them, He wouldn't have let them be kidnapped in the first place.

When they arrived at her parents' house she saw her brother Martin and his wife Stephanie and their baby in a stroller waiting for them. Her mother had told her they had gone to church with Stephanie's parents. They both worked for the same accounting firm, where they had met, and they had been married for two years. Since her mother had worried that Martin would never get married, the lucky girl could do no wrong, even in the kitchen. And she was a nice, earnest young woman, perfect for Martin.

Before her father could let them into the house, Martin asked: "Where's Amanda?"

"I'll tell you when we get inside," Carol said.

She waited until they were alone in the kitchen with their mother, who was busy at the stove, and then she told him what had happened.

Martin listened, and when she had finished he didn't say a word. He stepped toward her and put his arms around her and hugged her tight, which wasn't like him. Martin had always shied away from the hugs of his mother and his sisters.

When they stepped apart he asked: "Is there anything I can do to help?"

"I can't think of anything. But if I do, I'll let you know."

The feast began with an antipasto of mozzarella, red peppers, artichoke hearts, prosciutto, olives, and sopresata. That was followed by broccoli rabe and sausage, and then rigatoni with meat sauce, and then filet of sole coated with bread crumbs and lightly fried, and then roast chicken with a scent of lemon, and finally Tiramisu for dessert. Her mother had made everything except the dessert, which she had bought at a pastry shop near Arthur Avenue.

Carol tried to eat the food, but the only thing that went down was a slice of chicken breast. They went home with plenty of leftovers.

On Monday morning they left the house in their usual sequence. First, Matthew left for school, a five-minute walk. Then Brian left for his office in the village, where he would make coffee for the three people who worked for him. And finally Carol left for the college, a ten-minute drive at most, depending on the traffic lights.

She had graduated from St. Catherine twenty years ago with a degree in marketing and the dream of working for an advertising firm on Madison Avenue. She hadn't found a job in advertising, but she had found one in public relations, and she had met Brian while doing publicity for a major project of the firm he worked for. A year later they got married, and within a few months she was pregnant with Matthew. Since their one-bedroom apartment wouldn't be large enough for a family, and since they couldn't afford to buy a large enough apartment in the city, they bought the house in Hastings, which they restored, and after two years of commuting to the city Brian left the firm and started his own business in Hastings.

Carol had interrupted her career to raise her children until they were both in school, and then instead of getting a job in the city she limited her options to a job that wasn't more than ten minutes from where they lived. She immediately thought of seeing what might be available at St. Catherine, and she found a position there as assistant to the director of public relations. Her current position was assistant vice president for institutional advancement, a bureaucratic term for fund raising. She was responsible for major events and alumni relations, and when she had left for vacation everything was in place for one of the major events of the year—the Trustees' Dinner. So her main reason for not waiting until the next day to report to work was to make sure everything was still in place.

After backing out of their driveway she drove to North Street, where she turned left, and then she turned right onto Warburton Avenue. She went only as far as Villard Avenue, where she turned left and went up the hill to Broadway. She made the light and turned right onto Broadway, but she didn't make the light at Five Corners, and it was a long one.

While she was waiting for it to change, her phone rang. It was inside her handbag, and usually when she was in the car she didn't answer it, but in the present situation she didn't want to miss a phone call. Maybe it was a kidnapper asking for ransom, or maybe it was Ramsey with some good news. So she dug out her phone with an eye on the traffic light hoping for once it wouldn't change for a while.

The caller identification didn't say who it was, but the area code was New York City. She pressed the button for receiving calls and said: "Hello?"

"Mrs. Delaney?" It was a woman's voice.

"Yes. I'm in my car now, waiting for a light. Who's calling?"

"I'm calling for Mr. Catena at the New York office of the FBI. He would like to meet with you and your husband as soon as possible."

"What about?" she asked cautiously.

"Your daughter Amanda."

At that moment the light changed to green and the driver behind her beeped his horn.

"I'll call you right back," she told the woman. She pressed the button to end the call and turned right onto Main Street and then into the A&P parking lot, where she stopped the car and pressed the buttons to return the call.

"Federal Bureau of Investigation, Elizabeth Hargesheimer speaking. How can I help you?"

"This is Carol Delaney calling you back."

"Oh, thank you, Mrs. Delaney. Can you meet with Mr. Catena today?"

"Yes, of course. Where's your office?"

"We're at 26 Federal Plaza. Do you know where that is?"

"Yes. What floor are you on?"

Elizabeth told her, and they scheduled a meeting for eleven thirty, which gave her time to call her office, alert Brian, and make the ten-twenty local. Before ending the call she asked if there was any news, and Elizabeth said there wasn't, but they were working on the case and would do everything possible to solve it.

She left the A&P and drove back to the street where they lived. Like other streets in the center of town it was lined with old houses, some of them from the Victorian era. From this location they could easily walk to the schools, the church, the supermarket, the hardware store, the family doctor, the dentist, the post office, the dry cleaner, the library, the village hall, the service station, the railroad station, and five restaurants including a diner. The convenience had attracted her, and the old house had attracted Brian.

When she called her office to say she wouldn't be in that day her boss, Tom, got on the phone and good-naturedly kidded her about extending her vacation. She went along with him, not yet ready to tell him or anyone at work what had happened. They might have already heard about it on the news, but Tom obviously hadn't heard about it or he wouldn't have joked about her taking another day off.

Then she called Brian, and they arranged for her to drop by his office on the way to the train station. He was waiting outside the door for her, and they walked down the hill to the station feeling positive about the fact that the FBI was involved.

"Will the Walkers be there?" Brian asked as they walked across the pedestrian bridge to the track for the trains going to New York.

"I don't know. She didn't say."

"Well, maybe they want to talk with us one family at a time."

"I hope they do," Carol said, remembering how Richard had behaved in their meetings with Ramsey.

The train was on time, and they arrived at Grand Central shortly after eleven. They took the subway to Brooklyn Bridge and walked up Lafayette Street to Federal Plaza. It took them a while to clear security and gain access to the building, but over the years since 9/11 they had become used to it. The worst had been the period when you needed to clear security to attend a concert at Carnegie Hall.

Mr. Catena's office was on an upper floor, and he didn't keep them waiting. A serious young woman in a blue suit introduced herself as Elizabeth and led them into an office that was just big enough to hold a meeting with four people.

"Frank Catena," the agent said, shaking her hand as if she was in the receiving line of a wake. He was a lean man with closely cut dark hair and a rueful look in his dark eyes. He could have been her younger brother. "Please call me Frank."

At his invitation she and Brian sat down in the two substantial chairs while Frank and Elizabeth pulled up the two light chairs.

"Just so you know," Frank told them, "I'm going to meet with your friends, the Walkers, this afternoon. I wanted to meet with you separately."

"That's fine," Brian told him without making any further comment.

"If you'll bear with me, I'd like to verify the information I received from our embassy in Barbados." Frank asked the questions they had already answered for Ramsey, and Elizabeth recorded the information on an electronic tablet. Then he said: "Now, tell me about Amanda. How would you describe her?"

"She has red hair and green eyes—"

Frank waved his hand. "We have a physical description, and we have a picture. I want you to describe her personality."

"Well, she's lively, and she's friendly—"

"Is she friendly with strangers?"

"No. We warned her about talking with strangers. But she

doesn't have much experience with strangers," Carol added. "We live in a small village where we know everyone."

"Would you say she's been sheltered?"

"I guess she has been. I grew up in a tough neighborhood, and I didn't want that for her."

"I understand. Does she have a boyfriend?"

"No. She's only twelve."

"Does she like boys?"

"She'd rather be with girls. She thinks boys are dumb."

"The boys her age *are* dumb," Brian said.

"Does she get along with her older brother?"

"Yeah," Carol said. "They fought when they were younger, but they're fine now."

"What kind of relationship does she have with you?" Frank asked Brian.

"A good one, I think. I'm soft on her because she's a girl. I'm like the other fathers I know who are soft on their daughters."

"Are there discipline problems?"

"No, not really. She just doesn't always do what she's told."

"What kind of things doesn't she do?"

"She doesn't make her bed or clean her room," Carol said. "And she doesn't take showers. But other than those things she does what she's told."

"She always does her homework," Brian said.

"Is she a good student?"

"She's not a star," Carol said, "but she's above average. And she has a lot of friends."

"Is she popular?"

"Yes. She's outgoing, and she has a lot of empathy. The other girls talk with her when they have problems."

"Does she talk with you when she has problems?"

"She talks with both of us, depending on the problem."

"If it's a girl thing," Brian said, "she talks with Carol. If it's not, she talks with me."

Frank nodded. "How far along is your daughter with the girl things?"

"Not very far," Carol said. "There are almost no signs of puberty if that's what you mean."

"That's what I meant," Frank said gently. "I'm sorry I have to ask these questions."

"It's all right. I think I know where you're going."

"Does she know much about sex?"

"She's never asked about it," Carol said. "I'm sure she's learned about it from the internet, but she's still at the stage where it's theoretical."

"Would you say she's innocent?"

"Oh, yes. She's as innocent as a lamb."

Frank was silent with a look of sadness in his dark eyes, and then he said: "Tell me what your daughter likes to eat."

"She likes hamburgers, and fried fish, and crisp tacos, and egg rolls—"

"She likes anything with sugar in it," Brian said fondly. "And she loves ice cream."

"What kind of music does she like?"

"The music all the kids like," Carol said.

"She likes Katy Perry, and Taylor Swift, and Britney Spears," Brian said.

"What kind of clothes does she like?"

"If she had her choice," Carol said, "she'd only wear jeans."

"With holes in the knees," Brian added.

"What kind of toys does she like?"

"She likes her computer," Carol said.

"Like all the kids, she's addicted to it," Brian said.

"What about non-electronic things?"

"She still has a bear," Carol said.

"What's its name?"

"Bo." At that trigger she began to cry, and the tears streamed faster than she could wipe them away.

Brian reached over and tenderly put his hand on her shoulder.

"We've talked about your daughter enough," Frank said after a pause. "Now, let's talk about the situation."

Carol braced herself.

"It's been a week since the girls went missing, and if they were being held for ransom, we should have heard from the kidnappers by now. So we're leaning toward the theory of Detective Ramsey—"

"You talked with him?"

"More than once. And we think he's on the right track." Frank looked at her sympathetically. "How much do you know about human trafficking?"

"Not much," Carol said. "I was aware of it, but I didn't think it had anything to do with us."

"Most people don't, so you shouldn't feel bad for thinking that way. But the fact is, there are millions of girls around the world who are sex slaves. And most of them are between the ages of twelve and fourteen."

"That's disgusting," Brian said.

"It *is* disgusting," Frank agreed, "but it's a fact. And it's one of the main sources of income for organizations that are involved in drug dealing, money laundering, identity theft, computer hacking, extortion, and other criminal activities."

"Not to mention terrorism," Elizabeth said, speaking for the first time.

"In the old days when people talked about organized crime, they meant the Mafia, but they were small potatoes compared with the organizations today."

"Who are they?" Brian asked.

"They're Russians, Chinese, Americans, Europeans, Latin Americans— They're global in scope, and they're bigger than most legitimate business organizations."

"There are Russians on St. Anselm," Carol said, "who Detective Ramsey suspects of taking the girls off the island."

"I think he's right. I wish we could prove it."

"Do you think the Russians belong to a global organization?" Brian asked.

"I'm sure they do. I'm sure they're part of a global network for human trafficking."

"If they kidnapped the girls for that purpose," Carol said,

with a lump in her throat, "where would they take them?"

"They could take them to any big city," Frank said. "But they're not likely to bring them to New York. They're more likely to take them to a city in Asia."

"How would they get them there?" Brian asked.

"By a regular commercial flight. They'd create false identities and counterfeit passports."

"I assume the airlines are watching for them."

"They are. The girls are on a list with their pictures. But I have to remind you," Frank added, "these organizations have a lot of money."

"You mean to bribe people with."

"That's right. So they could easily slip the girls through the checkpoints."

"And then what? Where would you look for them?"

"We'd look for them wherever men go for commercial sex."

"You mean the local police would look for them."

"Yes. We'd rely on the local police."

"But as you said," Brian said, sounding discouraged, "these organizations have a lot of money. So they could bribe the local police."

"They could, and unfortunately they sometimes do—even in this country."

"Then how the hell do you fight them?"

"We fight them one case at a time," Frank said steadfastly. "And we work with people like Detective Ramsey who share our mission."

At their first opportunity to talk in private, which occurred after they left the building, they agreed that they liked Frank and had confidence in him. But at the same time they felt worse about the situation.

They were able to make the one-twenty local to Hastings, and on the train they shared a ham and cheese sandwich they had bought in the food court at Grand Central. They arrived in Hastings around two, and after walking up the hill from the station, which never got easier, they parted at Spring Street, with Brian heading toward his office and Carol toward home.

As she walked along Maple Avenue she debated whether to go to the college if only for an hour to see what was happening. Matthew would be getting out of school soon, and if he was planning to come right home, she wanted to be there. At breakfast he had seemed to be coping with the situation, but he was only fourteen and he had never dealt with anything like this, so there was no way of knowing how it would affect him.

When she reached their house she checked for mail before going in. It hadn't been delivered yet, which meant there was a substitute mailman today. Inside, she wandered through the hall and into the kitchen, where she killed some time putting away the dishes from breakfast. Then she sent a text message to Matthew, asking: "What are you doing after school?"

Within a minute he replied: "I'm going to Jeff's house."

"Okay," she texted. "Be home by five thirty."

"Okay," he replied instantly.

Jeff was the boy he had gone skiing with, and Jeff's mother worked at home as a freelance writer, so the boys wouldn't be alone. They would probably spend the rest of the afternoon in the basement playing computer games.

Since she didn't have to be at home for Matthew, she decided to make an appearance at the college. She drove over to Broadway, where she just missed the light. While she was waiting for it to change she imagined her daughter in the cabin of a boat with her hands tied behind her and two huge guys with shaved heads threatening her with a cruel punishment if she disobeyed them. It made Carol feel as if she had been injected with a lethal drug that was designed to maximize the agony of the person being executed.

The car behind her beeped, drawing her attention to the fact that the light had changed, and she took her foot off the brake.

The college was about five minutes south of Five Corners. It was on what had been the Morrissey estate, which at the time of its bequeathal to the Sisters of the Redemption had consisted of eighty acres and a mansion built of gray stone. The land was still intact, though now there were several buildings including another dormitory under construction, and the mansion still looked the same from the outside, though now it was reconfigured on the inside to provide offices for the president, the provost, and institutional advancement.

Carol's job at the college didn't pay her anywhere near what her last job in the city had paid her, but it gave her a lot more satisfaction. By helping the college raise money she enabled it to fulfill its mission of providing a high-quality private education to people who could not otherwise afford one. About a third of the students had their tuition covered by government grants and college aid, so their education was basically free, while the others paid what they could afford. The college prided itself on the fact that unlike graduates of most other colleges its graduates either had no loans or had relatively small loans. Carol had graduated from St. Catherine owing no money for student loans, so her commitment to the college's mission was grounded in her own experience, and her job satisfaction came from knowing that every dollar she raised went to help students from families like hers who lived in Yonkers, Mt. Vernon, or the Bronx.

On entering their office the first person she saw was Griselda, a bubbly young woman who worked for her, a graduate of the college's program in communications. Her parents were from the Dominican Republic so she was bilingual, which helped in many situations.

"I'm sorry," Griselda murmured, revealing that she knew about the kidnapping.

"How did you hear about it?" Carol asked her.

"From the news. It was on the Spanish channel my mother watches."

"Does Tom know?"

"I don't think he does."

"Well, I guess I better tell him." Sooner or later he would hear about it from the news, and it would be better if he heard about it first from her. "Is he here?"

"No. He's in a meeting with the president. But he should be back pretty soon."

While she waited for Tom to return from his meeting she reviewed the status of their projects, and she was relieved to learn from Griselda that everything was still in place.

They had finished their review when Tom appeared. As usual he was wearing a suit that fit him perfectly, with a dazzling white shirt and a blue tie. His hair was neatly combed and his face was cleanly shaven.

"Welcome back," Tom said, smiling. "I'm glad to see you, but I thought you were going to take another day of vacation."

"I only came in to check on things," Carol said. "I could have taken another week. Griselda has everything under control."

"Oh, I wouldn't go that far," Griselda said modestly.

"I would," Tom said. "Carol trained you well."

"I need to talk with you," Carol told him.

"Sure. Come in." He headed for his office, and she followed him, preparing herself.

With the door closed behind her, Carol said: "I guess you didn't hear about it from the news."

"Hear about what?" He was lowering himself into the chair behind his desk.

"My daughter and her friend were kidnapped."

"What?" He looked at her blankly as if he hadn't understood.

"They were taken off the island, and they're being held for some purpose, maybe for ransom but we don't know. We haven't heard from the kidnappers."

"While you were on St. Anselm," Tom said, blinking his eyes, "your daughter and her friend were *kidnapped?*"

"Yeah. I still don't believe it," Carol said. "But it happened. And to say the least, it's going to distract me from my job."

"Would you like to have some time off?"

"It depends on what happens. We're waiting to hear from the FBI, and if they find the girls we'll go and get them."

Tom nodded, still blinking his eyes. "Of course you can have time off for that."

"But while we're waiting I need to keep busy or I'll go crazy."

"You can do as much or as little as you want."

"Thanks. I'll do the best I can."

"I know you will." He stared across the room as if he was seeing a different world. "I can't imagine how I'd feel if that happened to one of my kids."

"I can't tell you how it feels. I can only tell you it's my worst nightmare."

He pressed his fingers against his eyes, and when he pulled them away she noticed that the tips were wet. Exhaling, he said: "I'll pray for them."

When she got home she saw the light flashing on the phone in the kitchen, which meant there was a message. She prayed that it was good news.

"Hello," a chirpy young woman said, "this is Lindsey Whalen at Channel 12 News. We'd like to do an interview with you. Could you call me back?"

Since she didn't get the number the first time, she played the message over.

So the word was out, and it wouldn't be long before everyone knew about the kidnapping. She could see how the publicity might help the search, but she was concerned about how it might affect Matthew, who should have been home by how.

She texted him, asking: "Where are you?"

Within a minute he replied: "I'm on my way home. Don't worry."

"Okay," she texted, realizing that she couldn't make up for taking her eyes off Amanda by watching Matthew too closely.

She was still in the kitchen, trying to figure out what to make for dinner, when Matthew appeared. She reminded herself not to smother him with protection, but after pausing for only a moment he came to her and put his arms around her and pressed his face against her, crying: "Oh, mom. I'm so worried about Amanda."

"I am too," she said, holding him.

"I'm praying for her."

"That helps."

"But what if they never find her?" he asked, drawing back his head and appealing to her with tearful eyes.

"They'll find her," she assured him, believing it.

"Well, I hope it doesn't take them long."

"I do too." The longer it took, the more damage could be done to her.

SIX

SHE HADN'T FELT like food shopping, and there weren't any leftovers, so she decided to make pasta for dinner. They always had boxes of pasta on hand, and she found a package of meatballs in the freezer compartment, a can of whole tomatoes in the pantry, a chunk of Parmesan cheese in the refrigerator, and a few cloves of garlic in the colander. With those ingredients she began to prepare spaghetti with meatballs, conscious of the fact that her mother would have made the meatballs from scratch.

She had dinner under way when Brian came home, no later than usual even though he must have had a lot to catch up on. In this situation other men might have escaped into their work, but here he was, as if to let her know he had no attention of doing that. As usual they gave each other a hug, but today it was longer and closer.

Before they asked Matthew to come down from his room, where he had retreated to escape into the virtual world, she told Brian about the call from Channel 12 News.

"How do you feel about it?" he asked, standing by the table.

"If it's on Channel 12 News, then everyone will know about it, and I'm concerned about how it might affect Matthew."

"How's he doing?"

"I think it's really hit him."

"But his friends don't know about it."

"I don't think so. Tom didn't know about it. But Griselda did. It was on the Spanish channel her mother watches."

"If it was on the Spanish channel," Brian said, still standing, "it's going to be on Channel 12 News whether or not we talk with them."

"I guess it will be. And the publicity might help the search."

"That was why we decided to talk with the reporter on the island."

After stirring the sauce with the wooden spoon she always used with the enamel pot, Carol said: "We should ask Frank if he thinks it might help."

"Okay," Brian said. "We can talk with him in the morning. Now, what about the Walkers?"

"We should talk with them tonight. Channel 12 must have called them too."

"You didn't hear from Donna?"

"No. But I only got the message when I came home from work, so she might not have had a chance to call me about it."

"Well, I think we should talk with them anyway."

"I think we should," Carol agreed. "I want to share what we learned from Frank."

"I want to make sure we're all together," Brian said.

"I think you and I and Donna are together."

"You have doubts about Richard?"

"I've always had doubts about Richard. And now that we're in a crisis with him—" She didn't have to finish the thought.

"It's not bringing out the best in him," Brian said. "But we need to have him onboard."

Since the water in the large pot was boiling, she opened a box of spaghetti and poured the contents into the pot. A half pound of pasta was more than enough for her and Brian, but Matthew could easily put away a half pound, so she needed the whole box. "Well, what if we decide to talk with Channel 12 and Richard decides not to?"

"That's what I mean by having him onboard."

"But if he decides not to, should we do it without them?"

"I think we should. I mean if Frank thinks it's a good idea."

Carol stirred the pasta with the long plastic fork that could have been used as a back scratcher, separating the noodles. "This is going to be ready soon. Could you call Matthew?"

As he left the kitchen Brian said: "We'll have to talk with him about it."

"We can do that after we talk with the Walkers." On a tine of the fork she delicately lifted a noodle out of the pot and tested it for doneness.

During dinner, which they ate as usual at the kitchen table, they talked about the prospects of the Yankees, who were going to play their opening game in five days. Brian had grown up in Mystic, Connecticut, within the territory known as the Red Sox Nation but not in the heart of it, and he had been exposed to a lot of people from New York while working in his parents' restaurant, so it hadn't been difficult for him to switch his allegiance to the Yankees for the sake of his wife and children. Matthew was passionate about baseball, and he had played on organized teams since Little League in more than one position, though he was now committed to playing shortstop like Derek Jeter. The best thing about the conversation was that at least for a while it seemed to take his mind off the plight of his sister.

Meanwhile, Carol had called Donna and arranged a meeting at the Walkers' house around eight thirty, so as soon as they had cleaned up the kitchen she and Brian headed there. The Walkers lived less than a half mile away, but their house was on the top of the hill, and since she didn't feel like climbing it on a stomach filled with spaghetti and meatballs, they took Brian's car, which was behind hers in the driveway.

There were all types of houses up on the hill, which back in the days when Hastings was a factory town was where the owners and managers lived. It was still an area where the more affluent people lived, and in some people's minds it had more status than the area where Carol and Brian lived. But in their minds the true aristocrats of the village were people who had been born there and served in the volunteer fire department, including people whose families had lived there for generations. Though Carol lived among people in this group, she had no pretensions about belonging to it—their house was still referred to by the name of the family that had built it a hundred and seventy years ago.

The Walkers' house was less than thirty years old, and at times Carol envied its newness, especially features like its three full bathrooms, its family room, and its laundry room next to the kitchen, but she wouldn't have wanted to live there since it wasn't a convenient location.

Donna greeted them at the door, and she led them into the den, where Richard was sitting in one of the brown leather easy chairs. He got up and welcomed them and asked them what they would like to drink.

"I'll have a white wine," Carol said since she had noticed that Donna was having wine.

"I'm having a single malt," Richard told Brian. "Would you like some?"

"No, thanks. But if you have a beer, I'd like one."

"I have Stella. Is that okay?"

"Sure. Whatever you have is fine."

While Carol and Brian sat down on the brown leather sofa Richard went to a wood-paneled refrigerator that was built into the room, and he got out a beer and a bottle of wine. While he was pouring the wine he asked: "What did you think of Frank Catena?"

"I liked him," Brian said.

"Do you think he has the experience to handle this case?"

"I think he does. We didn't ask him about his experience, but he acted like he knew what he was doing."

"I thought he was all right," Richard said, handing the glass to Carol. "But I'm checking on him, just to make sure."

"I have a good feeling about him," Carol said.

"There you go again with your feelings," Richard said, opening the bottle of beer.

"My feelings are usually right."

"Well, I hope they're right about Catena." Richard poured the beer into a pilsner glass. "So far we haven't gotten much from Ramsey."

Changing the subject, Brian asked: "Did you get a call from Channel 12 News?"

"We did," Donna said. "A woman named Lindsey Whalen called. She wants to interview us about the girls."

"Are you going to talk with them?"

"I'd rather not," Richard said. "I didn't mind the story on the island television, but everyone in Westchester would see this story, and that would be the end of our privacy."

"It would be hard for Jennifer," Donna said, referring to Stacy's younger sister.

"It would also be hard for Matthew," Carol pointed out.

"Then why on earth would we want to do it?" Richard asked, handing the glass to Brian.

"Whether or not we talk with them," Brian said, "they're going to do a story about it. And if we talk with them, we can shape the story."

"They'll do whatever they want with the story," Richard said.

"Still, the publicity might help the search," Carol said.

"It might, but it might not. If they announce the reward, then every nut in the county will be calling the FBI with a lead."

"The whole purpose of the reward was to get leads."

"But that was in a targeted area, where someone might have seen what happened. No one in Westchester will have any useful information."

"The story will go beyond Westchester."

"It'll go everywhere in the world," Brian said.

"But we don't want the police searching everywhere in the world," Richard argued. "We want them searching in the Caribbean."

"How do we know the girls are still in the Caribbean?"

"We don't. But they couldn't have gone very far in a boat."

"Frank said that whoever took them could put them on a commercial flight."

"I know," Richard said. "But I got the impression he doesn't think they've done that yet. It takes time to create a false identity and a counterfeit passport."

"I didn't get the same impression. But even if they're still in the Caribbean, this story could reach more people there."

"And that outweighs my concern for Matthew," Carol said. "I know the publicity will be hard for him, but sooner or later everyone in the county is going to know about the kidnapping, and the sooner we get the publicity this story could give us, the sooner we might find the girls."

"Well, let's ask Frank and see what he thinks," Richard said.

"We plan to call him in the morning," Brian said. "So if he thinks it's a good idea, will you go along with us?"

"I will," Donna said, coming around.

"Then I will," Richard said as if he had no choice.

Carol was relieved since she had been afraid that Richard would find another reason not to do it. By then, as a result of arguing with him, she had moved into a position of being strongly in favor of doing the interview, though of course they would be guided by Frank.

When they got home she headed upstairs to talk with Matthew since they had agreed that in this situation it was better for one of them to talk with him than to double-team him. She expected to find him in his room, sitting on his bed and playing on his computer. There were times when she regretted yielding to her children on the issue of whether they should have computers, which she had finally done after verifying their arguments that all the other kids had them. Though neither of her children spent an excessive amount of time online since they were conscientious students and enthusiastic athletes, still the hours they spent in the virtual world were hours missed in the real world, and as she headed down the hall toward Matthew's room she wondered if the girls might have avoided getting into trouble if they had been exposed to the real world where she had grown up. With a pang she remembered Frank asking if Amanda had been sheltered and her mother implying she had been.

As usual the door of Matthew's room was open, which gratified her since she had heard other parents complain about their children closing the door when they were online as if they didn't want their parents to know what they were up to.

91

She found Matthew sitting cross-legged on his bed with his computer in his lap.

"Hi, mom," he said without looking up from the screen.

"Hi, honey," she said. "How are you doing?"

"I'm doing okay." Matthew stopped playing and gave her his attention.

She sat down on the edge of his blanket. "I need to ask you something, okay?"

"Okay," he said warily.

"Channel 12 News wants to do a story about Amanda and Stacy. They'd interview me and your father, and they'd put us on the news. So everyone at school would know about what happened to your sister."

"I haven't told anyone about it."

"I know you haven't. And if I had my way," she said, "I wouldn't want anyone in town to know about it. But this is an opportunity to help the police find the girls."

"How would it help them?"

"By letting the whole world know about it. The story would show their pictures, and maybe someone would recognize them and call the police."

Matthew nodded as if he understood. "So everyone at school would know about it."

"They would, and most people would be nice about it. But some people might say bad things about your sister."

"If they said anything bad about her, I'd pound them."

"You're a good brother," Carol said, patting his shoulder. "But you wouldn't have to pound them. You'd just have to ignore them."

Matthew considered. "Well, if it'll help the police find Amanda, I can handle it. That's what you wanted to ask me, isn't it?"

"I know you can handle it. I wanted to ask you if you're ready to handle it."

"Yeah, I'm ready," Matthew said. "But I still can't believe my sister was kidnapped."

"I can't either. I keep hoping I'll wake up and find that it was only a nightmare. But it wasn't. It really happened. And with your help we can handle it."

He extended his open palm to her in a consolatory hi-five gesture.

She pressed her palm against his and put her other arm around him and softly kissed his head, saying: "I love you."

"I love you too, mom."

The next morning they called Frank, with her on the upstairs phone and Brian on the downstairs phone. It was easier than trying to do a conference call with their cell phones.

Elizabeth answered and asked them to wait while she found Frank.

When he got on the line Brian told him about the call from Channel 12 News and asked him what he thought about it.

"I think it could help us," Frank said. "They can sell this story, so it'll go everywhere."

"Do you see any downside?"

"Only for you. Are you ready to handle the publicity?"

"We think we are," Carol said. "But we've never been in this situation before."

"Most people haven't been, thank God."

"If we say we're offering a reward," Brian said, "should we tell people to call your office?"

"I'll give you a number they can call. And don't worry, we can handle it."

"What about the Russians? Should we talk about them?"

"I don't know why not. It could put some pressure on them," Frank said, "and when people feel pressure they make mistakes."

"Is there anything we shouldn't talk about?" Carol asked.

"I can't think of anything. If you talk about what you know, and what you think, and what you feel, you'll be fine."

"Okay. We'll do the interview," Brian said. "We'll let you know when they're going to air it."

"If you call them now, they'll air it this evening. It's a big story."

She went downstairs and joined Brian in the kitchen, where she called Donna and let her know that Frank was in favor of their doing the interview. After relaying this information to her husband, Donna asked her to coordinate things, so Carol called the number that Lindsey Whalen had left yesterday.

It took only a half hour to arrange for the television crew to come to their house at ten that morning and to go to the Walkers' house at noon. So as Frank had guessed, the story was going to air that evening.

The television crew arrived on time. It consisted of Lindsey and a long-haired cameraman, who had a camcorder in one hand and a tripod in the other hand.

Lindsey was a natural blond with the type of hair that probably always looked good, even in the morning when she got up, and she had the energy of a cheerleader. But as soon as they got down to business she impressed Carol with her seriousness and her sensitivity.

The first decision was where to do the interview, and after considering the living room and the kitchen they decided on Amanda's bedroom, which would give viewers an intimate picture of the missing girl. When Lindsey had positioned her and Brian on the bed she asked: "Is there something of your daughter's that you could hold?"

"I could hold her bear," Carol said.

"A bear? That's perfect. We want viewers to realize how young she is."

Carol got up and went to their bedroom and retrieved Bo, explaining: "I've been sleeping with him. He smells like her."

"I understand," Lindsey said with moist eyes.

She sat down again on the bed while the cameraman set up his tripod several feet away.

"Try holding him in front of your tummy," Lindsey said.

"Like this?" she asked, with both hands on the bear.

"That's good. I gather your daughter's a Yankees fan."

"Oh, yeah. My son is too. They love Derek Jeter."

"Is the bear wearing a Jeter shirt?"

She turned Bo around, revealing Jeter's name and his number on the back.

"That's awesome. We should be able to use it somehow. Maybe we can get Derek to sponsor a campaign to find your daughter."

"We need all the help we can get," Brian said.

"Remember that line," Lindsey said.

When the cameraman was ready Lindsey sat down in front of them, taking the chair from Amanda's desk, and began the interview, saying: "Tell us what happened."

She exchanged a look with Brian, who indicated that she should tell it.

"For spring break," Carol began, "we planned to take our children to the island of St. Anselm, in the Caribbean, but our son was invited to go skiing with the family of a friend, so we took a friend of our daughter's with us. We were staying at an all-inclusive resort, and the girls were having a good time swimming and playing tennis. But one afternoon, for some reason, they left the resort."

"On their own?"

"Yeah. They were playing tennis, and we took our eyes off them for a while. And the next thing we knew, they were missing." She recounted how they had gone into town with the security guard looking for them, and how they had found the damaged phone. "So then we knew something had happened to them, and we called the police. They came right away, and after talking with some fishermen they concluded that the girls had been kidnapped and taken off the island in a yacht owned by Russians who live there."

"Did they pursue the yacht?"

"They had our ships go after it."

"What ships are you talking about?"

"The ships we deploy in our war on drugs."

"That's interesting," Lindsey said. "But it's another story. So did the ships catch the yacht?"

"They did, but the girls weren't on it. The police believe the

Russians knew our ships were after them, so they transferred the girls to another boat."

"How would they have known our ships were after them?"

"They could have intercepted the police communications," Brian said.

"Then they're not just people," Lindsey said, "who happen to live on the island."

"No. The police believe they're involved in criminal activities like drug dealing, money laundering, and human trafficking."

"Do they believe the girls were taken for a purpose other than ransom money?"

"They believe it's possible," Brian said grimly.

"Have you heard from the kidnappers?"

"No. We haven't," Carol said. "But if they want money, we'll pay them anything."

"I heard you're offering a reward," Lindsey said.

"We're offering a million dollars for information that enables us to find the girls."

"If you have such information, please call this number," Lindsey recorded for the viewers, and then she asked: "Is that your daughter's bear you're holding?"

Carol nodded, unable to speak.

"What's his name?"

"Bo. It doesn't mean anything." Carol let the tears flow. "It's just a word she liked to say when we gave him to her."

"How old was she then?"

"She was three."

"And how old is she now?"

"She's twelve now."

"Is there anything you'd like to say to our viewers?"

"Yes." She faced the camera and appealed to the people she imagined watching: "If you have our baby, please give her back. Or if you know what happened to her, please call."

"That's it," Lindsey said to the cameraman. She rose from the chair and came to Carol and put her arms around her, saying: "My heart's with you."

"Thank you," Carol said, wiping her eyes.

When the crew had left they gave themselves some time to recover and then they called the members of their families who didn't yet know what had happened, so they wouldn't hear about it first from the news. Brian called his parents in Fort Lauderdale and his sister in Providence. Carol called her sister in San Francisco. She woke Paula, who finally came out of a daze when she heard what had happened. Carol and her sister weren't close since Paula had always lived in another world, but this situation brought them together. Paula even offered to get on the next plane to New York, but Carol thanked her and told her it wasn't necessary.

Then they left the house and went to work. She had called and told Griselda she would be late, and it was almost noon when she arrived at the office.

As if he understood her need to keep busy, Tom gave her a data collection project that would occupy her for at least a week. She was able to lose herself in the task for periods of time, but then she was jolted by the image of Amanda with her hands tied behind her and the two huge men with shaved heads hovering over her.

Around one in the afternoon Tom persuaded her to join him and Griselda for lunch at Gianna's, a restaurant where they went regularly because it was nearby and the food was good. While they were eating they talked business, which distracted Carol's mind but didn't ease her heart. And she knew she was only going through the motions.

Back in the office, she called Donna to find out how their interview had gone.

"I liked Lindsey," Donna said. "I thought she was sensitive."

"I thought so too. How long did you talk with her?"

"About an hour. Richard did most of the talking."

"I hope he let you appeal to the viewers."

"He finally did. But it was hard."

"I know. For me it's getting harder."

"It's getting harder for me too, I guess because I'm realizing that I might never—" Donna broke off, sobbing.

"We're going to find them," Carol assured her, wanting to believe it.

She went back to the task of collecting data, but it didn't engage her as much as before, and she had to force herself to concentrate.

On her way home from the college she finally had a chance to stop at the A&P to buy food and replenish their stocks of household items. She had a list, which she had made while they were waiting for the television crew, and she pushed her cart up and down the aisles, taking the house brands when she had a choice. Out of habit she was a careful shopper, though now it seemed futile to save a few pennies on a bottle of catsup.

At the checkout counter she ran into a neighbor, who asked how her vacation was. She said it was fine, not wanting to talk about it and knowing the truth would come out that evening on Channel 12 News. Already she imagined the look of sympathy the neighbor would give her the next time they met.

Since the front door of their house was unlocked, she knew that Matthew was there. She had refrained from texting him to find out what he was doing after school, and she hoped he hadn't come right home and spent the rest of the afternoon there alone.

She was putting the groceries away when Brian came home, earlier than usual so he would be there when they aired the story. They usually watched the news late in the evening on the set in their bedroom, but tonight they would open the pine cabinet that hid the set in their living room and watch the news as a family.

It was almost six, so she didn't have time to get dinner under way before the news came on. They were having chicken, skinless and boneless breast grilled on top of the stove, with basmati rice and zucchini. She would flavor the chicken with lemon juice, the rice with butter, and the zucchini with garlic. Luckily, neither of her children was picky, so they all ate the same meal, unlike the families in which everyone ate a different meal.

And they ate healthy food, unlike the families that lived on takeout fast food or prepared meals heated in a microwave, though now it seemed futile to feed her family healthy food.

"I'll call Matthew," Brian said after checking the mail on the kitchen table.

"I'll be right with you," Carol said.

A few minutes later they were in the living room, sitting on the Persian rug that covered only the middle of the floor and left visible wide swaths of the original pine boards. The rug, which itself was thick, had a thick lining underneath it, so it was comfortable to sit on. That was how they watched television as a family, sitting on the floor.

Their story was the top item. Carol's first impression was how good Lindsey looked on the screen—and how tired she and Brian looked. She liked the way they had edited the interviews, alternating between the two couples. Though Richard had done most of the talking, they used more footage of Donna, whose tearful pleas would have moved the hardest heart. They showed the number for viewers to call if they had information about the girls, and they ended the story with Carol's appeal: "If you have our baby, please give her back. Or if you know what happened to her, please call."

"Oh, mom," Matthew cried, crawling into her arms.

She held him closely, stroking his hair.

"They did a good job," Brian said.

"They did," she agreed. "I hope it helps."

When she went to the college the next day and turned on her computer she found a large number of emails from people who worked there, including people she didn't even know. In one way or another they said: "You're in my prayers."

She was touched by this outpouring of concern, though it also made her not want to leave her office and face people. Luckily, none of the messages required a response except for the one from Sister Maura, one of the few nuns remaining from the time when St. Catherine had been a women's college. That was before

Carol had gone there. In fact, if it had still been a women's college then, she would have gone somewhere else.

The message from Sister Maura said: "Please call me."

She had taken a religion course with Sister Maura, and she had liked her as a teacher but she hadn't known her beyond that role until she came to work at the college, and then she had begun to see her regularly while organizing fund-raising events. Sister Maura had her own system for keeping in touch with alumni, and she seemed to know what every graduate of the college was doing, not only the women but also the men. She kept in especially close touch with the alumni who had been athletes, and she could tell you the batting averages of the three guys who were currently playing major league baseball.

Having been taught from an early age to always obey orders from nuns, Carol promptly called Sister Maura and made an appointment to see her at eleven.

Sister Maura's office was in Wagner Hall, in the school of liberal arts. She was back teaching religion now after serving as an administrator during a period when the nuns did battle with a board chairman who had wanted to sell the campus to a real estate developer, turn the college into a trade school, and move what was left of it to an office building in downtown Yonkers. Carol had lived through that period, and even though the chairman had tried to intimidate her, she had remained loyal to the nuns and their vision for the college. At one crucial point she had given them ammunition to use against him, letting them know that instead of giving a lot of money to the college as he claimed, he had given less than five thousand dollars.

Sister Maura was in her office, sitting at her desk. She had short wavy gray hair with streaks of black and acute gray eyes. In front of her blue sweater, hanging from a gold chain, was a gold cross—the only visible indication that this woman was a nun. On the desk lay a calendar turned to the month of April with some of the dates circled, presumably home games of the Yankees, which Sister Maura found easier to attend now that there was a train running from Yonkers to Yankee stadium.

"How are you doing?" Sister Maura asked, looking at her closely.

"Not well, sister," Carol said, sitting down in front of the desk where students who needed help sat, though as a student she had never sat there.

"You know you're in my prayers without my telling you, so that's not why I asked you to see me." Sister Maura paused. "I asked you to see me because your husband said in the interview that the people who took your daughter and her friend are involved in criminal activities like drug dealing, money laundering, and human trafficking."

"That's what the island police believe."

"Well, if the girls weren't kidnapped for ransom money, I know someone who might be able to help you find them."

"The FBI is searching for them."

"They're a fine organization," Sister Maura said. "We have a number of alumni with them. But the person I know runs an organization that specializes in human trafficking. And they've been successful in rescuing victims of trafficking."

"Are they in New York?"

"They're right here in Yonkers, but they work with other organizations that operate around the world."

"How do you happen to know them?"

"I got involved in this issue several years ago. I belong to a group of old nuns," Sister Maura explained with a faint self-deprecatory smile, "who have spent their lives working for peace and social justice. It's been a long road from the sit-ins and the antiwar protests to the issues of today. And we decided to make human trafficking our top priority."

"I can't bear to think about it," Carol said with her stomach churning. "It's bad enough not knowing what happened to them, but if they were taken for that purpose—"

"I won't pretend I know how you feel. I can only try to imagine how mothers feel when these things happen to their children."

"Why does God let them happen?"

"I don't know. And I won't tell you it's His plan."

"That's what our priest would tell me."

"Well, I'm not a priest. I'm only a nun."

Detecting irony in this statement, Carol said: "I have to admit I have trouble believing in a God who lets these things happen."

"I understand. But I think you know," Sister Maura said, "I'm not the type of person who waits for God to do something about a problem."

"I'm not either. So tell me how to contact this organization."

Sister Maura picked up a business card from the top of her desk and handed it to her, saying: "This is the person you should contact."

"Thanks, sister," Carol said, taking it. "And thanks for not giving me a load of—"

"Bullshit? I wouldn't do that. I wouldn't know how."

On her way home that evening Carol stopped in the village to pick up shirts from the dry cleaner and buy wine at the liquor store. She had been dealing with the owners of these stores for years, and she was on a friendly basis with them, so she was anxious about how they might react to the news of what had happened to her daughter. She was relieved when both the woman at the cleaner and the man at the liquor store didn't say anything about it but gave her silent looks of empathy.

At home she found Matthew in his room, playing on his computer.

"Have you done your homework?" she asked.

"Yeah. I didn't have much."

"So how was school?"

"It was all right."

"Did anyone say anything about your sister?"

"People said they were sorry," Matthew said, with his eyes still glued to the screen of his computer.

"I had the same experience at work."

"It didn't help, but at least it didn't make things worse."

She reached out and gently touched his shoulder, saying: "I understand."

She left him and changed out of her office clothes and went down to the kitchen to make dinner. Confronting that task, she decided to order pizzas instead. It usually took them about fifteen minutes, so she waited until Brian got home.

"How was your day?" he asked after their usual hug.

"Everyone was nice," she told him.

"They were nice at my office. I never realized how many people watch the local news."

"They probably didn't all see the story. One of them could have seen it and told the others."

"Yeah. Well, I hope it went out around the world."

Prompted by his last phrase, she said: "With all the other emails, I got a message from Sister Maura asking me to see her."

"Sister Maura? The nun you introduced me to at the Yankees game last summer?"

"Yeah. She heard what you said in the interview about the people who took the girls being involved in activities like drug dealing, money laundering, and human trafficking."

"Sister Maura doesn't miss a thing, does she," Brian said with admiration.

"Not only that, she cuts right through the bullshit. And based on what she knows about human trafficking, I think she's concluded that the girls were taken for that purpose."

"If she's right, she's way ahead of us."

"I know we're hoping the kidnappers will call us and demand money. But what if they don't? While we're waiting for them to call us, we're losing time."

"The FBI is searching for them. What else can we do?"

"Sister Maura told me about an organization that specializes in human trafficking. She said they've been successful in rescuing victims of trafficking. She gave me a person to contact there."

"Then we should contact them."

"I think we should. I just wanted to make sure you're with me on this."

"I'm with you all the way," Brian said, taking her hand. "No matter what happens."

Before she left for work the next morning her cell phone vibrated—it was on the kitchen table, where it made a sound like wood being drilled.

From the caller identification she knew it was Frank, and in her eagerness she fumbled on the buttons, accidentally cutting him off.

"I'm sorry," she said after calling him back. "I'm not good with these devices."

"That's okay," he said calmly. "I called to tell you they found Stacy."

"They did? Is she all right?"

"They say she is."

"What about Amanda?"

"She's still missing," Frank said. "But Stacy can give us information that'll help us find her. So this is good news."

It was good news in the sense that she no longer had to feel responsible for Stacy, and it was good news in the sense that Frank had said, so it gave her more hope of finding her daughter, but it didn't relieve her anxiety.

SEVEN

FRANK DIDN'T HAVE much information beyond the facts that Stacy was in Panama, she had escaped from the kidnappers, and she was being held for protection by the police. She wouldn't talk with the police, but she had asked them to call her parents, who were going to Panama to bring her home.

The police in Panama had notified Frank, who had notified Ramsey and other members of the search network. Frank expected that when Stacy was back at home she would give him the information he needed to arrest the Russians and find out where they had taken Amanda.

Carol called Brian at his office and let him know the good news. She could tell it raised his hope but didn't relieve his anxiety, as it hadn't with her. And then she called Donna on the chance that they hadn't yet left for Panama. She wanted not only to share a genuine feeling of happiness for her friend, but also to validate a feeling of absolution for the sin of taking her eyes off her friend's daughter.

She let the phone ring until she heard the voicemail, and she left the message: "I'm so happy for you, Donna."

Within a minute the kitchen phone rang, and assuming it was Donna she answered it.

"Hi. It's Lindsey," a chirpy voice said. "I heard the good news. I tried to reach the Walkers, but they're not answering, so I thought you might be able to give me some information."

"How did you hear about it?" Carol asked, playing for time.

"We usually don't reveal our sources, but I'll tell you. I heard about it from a journalist on St. Anselm."

"You mean Keith Hamilton?"

"Yes. He said you did an interview with him."

"We did. We thought the publicity might help the police."

"I think it will. It might have already helped them."

She wondered how Keith had heard about it, and then she decided Ramsey must have told him. It looked as if both Keith and Ramsey wanted to keep the story alive. "I don't have much information. I only know that Stacy's in Panama, she escaped from the kidnappers, and she's being held for protection by the police."

"That's what Keith told me. Did you hear about it from him or from another source?"

"I heard about it from another source."

"You did?" Lindsey said. "Then it's confirmed. Do you know if the Walkers are going to Panama to get their daughter?"

"I assume they are."

"You haven't talked with them?"

"I couldn't reach them."

"Well, I have enough to announce this development on the evening news," Lindsey said. "It won't be news to the kidnappers, but it might induce them to make a deal."

"What kind of deal?"

"They give back your daughter in return for leniency."

"But why would they be willing to do that now?"

"Now they know they're going to get caught. The police will have a witness who can identify them."

"I hope they react that way," Carol said, remembering what Brian had said about the kind of kidnapper they were dealing with.

"They will if they're rational," Lindsey said.

On Channel 12 News that evening they watched Lindsey announce that one of the missing girls had been found in Panama. The girl had escaped from the kidnappers and was being held for protection by the police. Her parents were on their way to Panama to bring her safely home. The police hoped she could provide information that would help them catch the people who had kidnapped the two girls. The other girl was still in their hands, and there was still a reward for information that enabled her parents to find her.

The next day was Good Friday, and they went to church in the afternoon. At one moment during the service Carol had the thought that if God would let his only Son die such an agonizing death, He wouldn't spare her daughter from suffering.

On Saturday Donna called her. They were back from Panama, and they wanted to meet with her and Brian that evening around nine. Since Donna wouldn't want to leave her girls alone for a minute, Carol agreed to go to the Walkers' house.

They went into the family room, and Richard offered Brian a single malt, which he declined for a beer. The girls were upstairs where they couldn't hear the conversation.

"How is she?" Carol asked when they were settled.

"Physically, she's fine," Richard said.

"We took her to the family doctor today," Donna said.

"Has she told you what happened?" Brian asked.

"At first she didn't want to talk about it," Richard said. "She was still in shock. But she finally opened up. She said they were at the harbor, looking out to sea, when two huge men appeared out of nowhere. She said Amanda tried to call you, but one of the men grabbed her phone and stomped on it. The other man pulled out a gun and made Stacy give him her phone. And then they made the girls go out onto the pier and get into the yacht."

"So Ramsey was right about what happened," Carol said.

"While one of the men held the gun on them, the other man started the yacht, and with the help of a third man, who was already on board, they headed out to sea. The girls were in the cabin, but they could hear the men talking in a language they didn't understand. At one point the men got very excited, and they changed course—"

"That must have been when they saw the fishing boat," Brian said, connecting what they knew.

"And later they heard them talking on the radio."

"That must have been when they were warned that our ships were after them."

"Within a half hour they transferred the girls to another boat, which had two men on board. They traveled through the night and in the morning they went into a harbor."

"I wonder where."

"She has no idea. They were taken to an airstrip and put into a small plane, which flew all day across the water and landed as it was getting dark."

"That must have been Panama."

"After telling the girls that if they called for help or tried to escape, they'd be shot dead, the men got them out of the plane and drove them to a hotel, where they tied them up in a hot room and held them for a few days. And then they brought them new clothes and new passports."

"Oh, my God," Carol said, hearing this evidence that the girls had been trafficked.

"They had checked out of the hotel," Richard continued, "and they were leaving when the deskman yelled after them. Both men turned around, and at that moment the girls ran. There were people on the street, so the men couldn't shoot them, but they ran after them. According to Stacy, they both would have gotten away, but Amanda stepped into a hole and sprained her ankle. Stacy stopped to help her, but Amanda told her to keep running, so she kept running. When she looked back she saw the men catch Amanda."

"Weren't there any police around?" Brian asked.

"If there were, they didn't pay attention. You know how they are in those countries."

"What did Stacy do then?" Carol asked.

"She asked for directions to the police station, and a nice woman took her there. She called us from the police station."

"Did she tell the police about the Russians?"

"She told them she'd been kidnapped," Richard said, "but she was afraid to tell them more. She thought they might turn her over to the Russians."

"Why did she think they might do that?"

"On her fake passport she had a Russian name."

"Which they gave her," Carol said, "so the man traveling with her could claim she was his daughter."

"Evidently," Richard said.

"Okay. I understand why she wouldn't talk with the police in Panama, but when is she going to talk with Frank?"

"She's going to talk with him on Monday."

"Why not sooner?" Brian asked.

"We have to give her time to recover."

"But while she's recovering they still have Amanda."

"We made an appointment," Richard said precisely, "for Stacy to talk with Frank on Monday. So don't worry. He'll get the information he needs."

Carol could see it wouldn't help to press them further. With their daughter safe at home they no longer felt the urgency she did. And though she believed she would have acted differently if their situations were reversed, she wasn't absolutely sure she would have. So she couldn't blame them.

They went to the noon mass on Easter. As the congregation sang the processional, which declared that Jesus Christ was risen today, alleluia, Carol was unable to feel what she was supposed to feel. Instead, she felt as if she had been sealed in a tomb with a heavy stone on top of it.

When they got home she noticed that the message light was flashing on the phone in the kitchen, and she saw from the area code that the call was from St. Anselm. Brian went upstairs to get on the line in the bedroom while Carol called the number.

Ramsey answered, and after they exchanged greetings he said: "Frank Catena is keeping me up to date on things. As soon as he gets the information from your daughter's friend, we can move on the Russians."

"Are they still on the island?" Brian asked eagerly.

"They're still on the island," Ramsey said, "living like kings."

"But they know Stacy can identify them."

"They don't seem to be worried about that. They must be

counting on our government to protect them. But there are limits to what our government can do, especially since we're having an election later this year."

"So you don't think your government will tie your hands?"

"Not if your government tells them not to. They give them more than the Russians do."

"Well, the Walkers told us they're going to let Stacy talk with Frank tomorrow."

"I know," Ramsey said. "I was hoping they'd let her talk with him sooner."

"We tried to get them to let her talk with Frank sooner," Brian said.

"They said they have to give her time to recover," Carol said.

"The girl has her whole life to recover," Ramsey muttered. "Anyway, I called to see if you found out anything from your friends."

"We did," Carol said. "They confirmed your theory."

Brian related what Richard had told them.

"It's exactly what we thought happened," Ramsey said but without any hint of satisfaction.

"With that information couldn't you arrest the Russians?" Carol asked.

"I wish I could, but it's information you heard from your friends who heard it from their daughter, so it's only hearsay. We have to get it directly from the girl. But it's helpful to know in advance what happened."

"Will you be able to arrest them tomorrow?"

"As soon as I hear from Frank, I will. And I can't wait," Ramsey added grimly.

Brian spent the rest of the afternoon in the backyard playing catch with Matthew and giving him practice in fielding grounders, while Carol sat at the kitchen table paying bills and reviewing their budget. They had put the vacation on their credit card, so they were going to have a much bigger bill than usual. In a moment of euphoria she had told Donna not to worry about paying for Stacy since Jeff's family was paying for Matthew, but now she wished she had asked Donna to contribute something since they were likely to have some unanticipated expenses, and now after what had happened she couldn't ask Donna to pay for Stacy's airfare.

She had hoped the task of paying bills would occupy her mind, but she was disrupted by images of what Richard had told them: the huge man grabbing Amanda's phone and stomping on it, the girls being forced at gunpoint to walk onto the pier and get into the yacht, and being transferred to another boat, and being put into a plane, and being tied up in a hotel room. She saw them making a run for it, and Amanda stepping into a hole. She winced at the pain Amanda must have felt spraining her ankle, and she groaned at the terror Amanda must have felt knowing she wasn't going to escape.

When she had finished she went upstairs and got the bags of summer clothes they had worn on vacation and carried them down into the basement, where the washer and the drier were. The first load included Amanda's clothes, except what she had been wearing to play tennis that day, and as Carol put the last top into the washer she paused to smell it, closing her eyes and evoking her daughter.

With a load of wash in the machine, she went upstairs and thought about what to have for supper. They usually ate light on Sunday evening, often having soup and salad. In the crisper of the refrigerator she found an onion, carrots, celery, zucchini, and a hunk of red cabbage. On a higher shelf in a plastic container she found the leftover tomato sauce from the pasta on Monday, and in the pantry she found a can of beef broth and a can of cannellini beans. So she had what she needed to make a *minestrone*, which both her children liked though it was a soup of vegetables. Amanda even asked her to make it.

She got out the Dutch oven she had bought years ago while living in the city and put it on the stove and poured some light olive oil into it. She followed her mother's recipe, cutting the vegetables into small pieces, sautéing the onion until it was wilted, adding finely chopped garlic, and then the carrots, celery, zucchini, and cabbage, and then a half cup of tomato sauce, and finally the broth. She brought the soup to a boil, and then she turned down the flame and set her timer to one hour, which was as far as it would go. It would take at least two hours for the soup to be done, and after the first hour she would put in the *cannellini* beans.

By this time the washer should have completed its last cycle, so she went back down into the basement and removed the sodden clothes and put them into the drier. She started the drier and dumped the second load of clothes into the washer. And then she went back up to the kitchen, where she checked the soup. It was coming along.

With nothing else to do for a while, she went out the back door and stood on the porch and watched Brian and Matthew tossing the baseball back and forth. Unusually, her husband was good at both baseball and tennis, so he could play the different sports favored by their children. She had played volleyball in high school, and she had been fairly good at it, but she hadn't ever played baseball and she hadn't played tennis until recently.

Watching her husband and her son, she remembered playing doubles at the resort with the girls against her and Brian. Since she was weaker than either Amanda and Stacy, they were evenly matched, and it had been fun. She also remembered peering out the window of their room and seeing the girls on the tennis court. It was the last time she had seen Amanda.

At dinner they talked about the Yankees. Though she hadn't played baseball, Carol had some knowledge of the sport, having heard her father and her brother talk about it. So as her husband and her son discussed the possibilities for the rotation now that Andy Pettitte was back on the team, she could follow them and even comment from time to time.

That night she lay awake worrying, as she had since the girls went missing, but she finally went to sleep out of exhaustion, and she dreamed about the wonderful vacation they were going to have on St. Anselm.

Carol was at work the next morning when her phone vibrated. From the caller identification she saw it was Frank, and she expected him to say that Stacy had given him the information he needed, and Ramsey had arrested the Russians.

Instead, he said: "We have a problem."

"What do you mean?" she asked, her hope falling.

"I can't explain over the phone. Could you and Brian come into the city and meet with me? I tried to reach him, but I only got his voicemail."

"I'll get him," she said, "and we'll take the next train."

She drove to his office and found him there, and they headed for the station, trying to make the eleven-twenty. She found a parking place on Southside and filled the meter with quarters in an effort to minimize the ticket she would get. After racing across the overpass and down the steps, they landed on the platform just as the train was coming in.

Elizabeth met them and led them into Frank's office, where they sat in the chairs they had taken at their first meeting.

"What's the problem?" Carol asked, ignoring formalities.

"The Walkers," Frank said through his teeth, "decided not to let their daughter talk with us."

"They didn't come here this morning?"

"No. Richard called me around nine and canceled the meeting."

"But how could they decide not to let their daughter talk with you?" Brian asked.

"They have a right not to let her talk with us. She's a minor."

"I know," Carol said, "but she's Amanda's friend. She should want to help us find Amanda."

"I'm sure she does want to help us. But her parents decided not to let her."

"Did they tell you why?"

"They didn't tell me. But I could tell from Richard's voice that he was afraid."

"Afraid of what? He has his daughter safe at home."

Frank rubbed his chin. "He may believe his daughter's not safe. He may have been threatened."

"You mean by the Russians?"

"Ramsey thinks they belong to a global organization, and they could have gotten someone here to threaten the Walkers."

"Did Richard tell you they were threatened?" Brian asked.

"No. He didn't," Frank said. "He didn't give me a reason why they wouldn't let their daughter talk with us. But I can't think of any other reason."

"This just isn't right," Carol said with rising anger. "Their daughter has information that could help us find our daughter, and they won't let her give it to you?"

"You can make them let her, can't you?" Brian said.

"Oh, I could charge them with obstructing an investigation," Frank said, "but even if I was successful it would take forever. Remember, he's a lawyer."

"So how do we get them to change their minds?"

"That's why I wanted to meet with you. I thought you might have an idea."

"They're our friends," Carol said. "We should be able to get them to help us."

"As I said, I'm sure they want to help you. But they're afraid."

"Then we have to stop them from being afraid. And you can do that by protecting them."

"I can give them bodyguards," Frank said. "But that might not stop them from being afraid."

"You only have to protect them long enough for Ramsey to arrest the kidnappers," Brian said. "If they've been caught, they won't have any reason to threaten the Walkers."

"You're right. At that point they'll have to find another way to escape from justice."

"You mean by corrupting the law enforcement process?"

114

Frank nodded. "They try to do that all the time."

"I hope you're not saying they could get away with it," Carol said, confronting a new set of fears.

"If we get Stacy to testify against them," Frank assured her, "they won't get away with it."

"So we should go and talk with the Walkers."

"Since they're your friends, they'll talk with you. And you can tell them I'll protect them."

"They'll want to hear it directly from you," Brian said.

"They will.," Frank said. "But you have to get them to talk with me as soon as possible."

"We saw them yesterday," Carol said, "and we heard what Stacy told them. We gave the information to Ramsey, but he said he couldn't use it because it was hearsay."

"If you heard it from the Walkers, who heard it from their daughter, we can't use it. But it could be helpful."

"Then we should tell you what Richard told us," Brian said.

While he relayed the information Elizabeth took notes on her tablet, and when he had finished Frank said: "Well, that confirms Ramsey's theory."

"I was surprised when Ramsey said the Russians were still on the island," Carol said. "I mean, they knew Stacy could identify them. But now I understand. They were planning to threaten the Walkers and stop Stacy from talking with you."

"They're probably feeling comfortable now," Frank said.

"If they're assuming that Stacy won't talk with you," Brian said, "and if we can get her parents to let her, then Ramsey can surprise them."

"So get her parents to let her talk with me."

"We'll do our best," Carol said.

On the train back to Hastings she called Donna at her work number but was told that Donna had taken the week off, so she called her at home. After several rings she got Donna's voicemail, and she left a message asking the Walkers to meet with them as soon as possible.

She got to work around twelve thirty. With Griselda's help she finalized some arrangements for the Trustees' Dinner, and she made some progress on the data collection. But the longer she waited for Donna to return her call, the more she was distracted by that not happening.

Before leaving work she called Donna again and left another message.

When she got home, after making sure that Matthew was all right, she called Brian.

"Donna hasn't returned my calls," she told him.

"I guess they don't want to talk with us," he said, annoyed.

"But they *have* to talk with us. They have information that will help us find Amanda."

After a silence Brian said: "We should go to their house and insist that they talk with us."

"Yeah, we should," Carol said.

"When do you think would be the best time?"

"For us the best time is right now. But for them it might be after dinner."

"When do they have dinner?"

"They usually eat around six thirty."

"Okay," Brian said. "If you don't hear from Donna, we'll go to their house around seven thirty."

By seven thirty she hadn't heard from Donna, so they drove up to the Walkers' house and rang the bell. It took a long time for someone to answer, and while they waited Carol was afraid that the Walkers wouldn't let them in. But finally Richard came to the door.

"I left two messages for Donna," she told him, "and I didn't hear from her."

With his face devoid of any expression Richard said: "We don't want to talk with you."

"But you have information that can help us find Amanda."

"Our daughter has that information, and she's not going to talk with anyone."

"You mean you're afraid to let her?" Brian said.

116

Richard's face changed, becoming more vulnerable. "Why would we be afraid to let her?"

"Because the Russians threatened you."

"They didn't threaten us," Richard said, but he looked around nervously as if he thought they were being observed.

"You're sure acting like they threatened you."

"Please let us alone," Richard said, trying to close the door.

In anticipation Brian had placed his foot on the threshold, stopping the door. "We're not going to let you alone until Stacy talks with Frank."

Richard looked around and said: "Let's talk inside."

They followed him into the family room.

"Donna's upstairs with Stacy," Richard told them. "You have no idea what this experience has done to our daughter."

"What about *our* daughter? What kind of experience do you think she's having now?"

"Well, it's not as if I don't care, but—"

"But what?" Brian prompted him.

Richard made a gesture entreating them to understand. "I have to think about my family."

"Your daughter's safe at home," Carol said. "Our daughter's still in their hands."

Richard slumped into one of the leather easy chairs, and staring morosely into space, he said: "On Sunday night we got a phone call, which Donna answered. It was a man, and he told her that if Stacy talked with anyone outside her family, they would not only kill Stacy but they would also kill Jennifer. And they would kill them in a way that made them suffer as much as possible."

"How do you know it wasn't a nut?" Brian asked.

"He knew something about Stacy that he couldn't have learned from the news stories."

"And what was that?" Carol asked.

Richard paused as if it was something so personal that he didn't want to reveal it. But he finally said: "It's a tattoo."

117

"Your daughter has a *tattoo?*"

"It's only a small one. It's on her shoulder," Richard said, putting the tips of his fingers on a spot above his left clavicle.

"How did she get it?"

"She went in a car with some older boys who were getting tattoos, and they talked her into it."

"But she's only twelve. She must have needed her parents' permission to get a tattoo."

"Legally, she does. But you know how those places are."

"Did she tell you where she got it?" Brian asked.

"No. She wouldn't tell us."

With this new information Carol was inclined to believe that it hadn't been Amanda's idea to leave the resort, and that made her feel less responsible for what had happened to Stacy.

"So it wasn't a nut," Brian said. "The man either saw her or he got this information from the men who kidnapped her."

"That's what I concluded," Richard said.

"This morning we talked with Frank," Carol said. "He said he figured they'd threatened you, and he said to tell you he'd protect your children."

"How could Frank protect them?"

"He'd give them bodyguards."

"Bodyguards?" Richard laughed derisively. "A lot of good they'd do. Would they follow our children everywhere? Would they go to class with them?"

"I imagine they'd keep a close watch on them," Carol said, conscious of not having done that with Amanda and Stacy.

"And how would we explain the bodyguards to our children?" Richard asked. "Would we tell them a Russian mob threatened to kill them?"

"You wouldn't have to tell them that," Brian said.

"You could tell them," Carol said, "you don't want to take any chances that they'll be kidnapped."

"Yeah," Richard said. "So for the rest of their lives they'll worry about being kidnapped?"

"It wouldn't be for the rest of their lives," Brian insisted. "If Stacy identifies the kidnappers then Ramsey can arrest them. And they won't have anything to gain by hurting your children."

"They could gain revenge."

"But that would be senseless."

"The whole thing is senseless," Richard said. "I mean, why are there organizations that kidnap children and turn them into sex slaves?"

"I don't know why, but there are," Carol said.

At that moment Donna appeared, looking distraught—and not glad to see them.

"What's happening?" Richard asked.

"She had a breakdown,'" Donna told him. "I think we should find another therapist."

"She's seeing a therapist?" Brian asked.

"Of course she is. She has post-traumatic stress disorder."

"I'm sorry," Carol said contritely.

Donna gave her a look that said she should be sorry, but she didn't say it.

"They want us to let Stacy talk with Frank," Richard told her.

"Talk with Frank? *And get both our children killed?*"

"Frank said he'd protect them."

"How could Frank protect them?"

"That's what I asked," Richard said. "They said he'd give our children bodyguards."

Donna shook her head. "That wouldn't make them safe."

"He thinks it would," Brian said. "And he has a lot more experience than we do."

"Can he *guarantee* the safety of our children?"

"I don't know. You could ask him."

"I know what he'd say. He'd say they'll be as safe as they ever were. But that's easy for him to say. They're not his children."

"If Stacy identifies the kidnappers," Brian repeated patiently, "then Ramsey can arrest them. And they won't have anything to gain by hurting your children."

"What if they get away?"

"They won't get away. They're still on the island, confident that your daughter won't talk with Frank. So Ramsey can surprise them."

Donna seemed to consider their request, but then she shook her head, saying: "I'm sorry, but I can't let her do it. I can't put my children at risk."

"What about Amanda?" Carol asked. "She's at risk."

"I didn't put her into that situation," Donna said without looking at her directly. "You were the one who took her eyes off them."

Wounded, Carol retorted: "It wasn't Amanda's idea to leave the resort."

"It was," Donna argued. "Stacy said it was Amanda's idea."

"And you believe her? A girl who has a *tattoo*?"

"You told them about it?" Donna said, turning anxiously toward Richard.

"I had to," Richard said. "They asked how we knew it wasn't a nut who called us."

"So you must have taken your eyes off her," Carol told Donna.

With this parting shot they left the Walkers in the family room and went through the hall and out of the house, into the cold damp evening.

As they drove away, Brian said: "That didn't go well. But I think we should keep trying with them. They're still our best hope."

"I agree," Carol said. "And I'm sorry I ended it that way with Donna."

"You were justified in saying it. She hit you first."

"I know she did. But I shouldn't have hit her back."

"I don't know anyone who could have resisted hitting her back, so don't blame yourself."

"I'll try not to. And anyway, it's not about me. It's about Amanda."

After a silence Brian said: "Well, maybe while we're trying to get them to let their daughter talk with Frank, we should contact the organization that Sister Maura told you about."

"I think we should. I'll call them tomorrow."

EIGHT

THE NEXT MORNING after Matthew had left for school she called the number on the card that Sister Maura had given her. It was only a little after eight, but since it was an 800 number she hoped someone might answer now. And someone did answer after only two rings.

"Metro Alliance," the voice of a young woman said. "How can I help you?"

"I'd like to speak with Jeanne Zaleski," Carol told her.

"Just a moment, please. I'll see if she's here."

Carol waited, and within a minute another voice said: "Jeanne Zaleski. How can I help you?"

"My name is Carol Delaney," Carol said. "I was referred to you by Sister Maura."

"Sister Maura?" Jeanne said as if the name meant a lot to her. "Are you a prospective donor or a prospective client?"

"A prospective client."

"I'm sorry," Jeanne said. "I have to split my time between raising money and serving people, which means I'm always changing hats."

"I understand. I work in fund raising at St. Catherine."

"Then you know what it's like asking people for money. If I had a choice, I'd spend all my time serving people, but we couldn't do anything without money." There was a pause, and then with her preferred hat on, Jeanne asked: "Would you like to meet with me?"

"I would—as soon as possible."

"Could you be here at nine?"

"This morning?"

"Yah. It sounds urgent."

"It *is* urgent. Your card says you're on Riverdale Avenue—"

"We are," Jeanne said. "We're near Hudson Street. You know where that is?"

"I think I do. It's near the YMCA."

"Right. You can probably park on the street, but if you can't you can park in the municipal lot."

After ending the call she called Tom and let him know she would be coming in late. He told her to take as much time as she needed.

She left the house at eight thirty to provide enough time to park and find Jeanne's building. Though she had grown up in Yonkers, she hadn't spent much time in the central downtown area near Getty Square since her family didn't have much reason to go there. They shopped for food along McLean Avenue, and when they shopped for clothes or household items they went to the Cross County Center. One of her few reasons for going to the downtown area had been to see the dentist, who had his office in a building with an elevator on Broadway, and she didn't have happy memories of those visits.

As she passed Dock Street, which led down to the Yonkers railroad station, she saw the progress they had made on the project to daylight the Saw Mill River. From a history course she knew that a Dutchman had built a saw mill not far from here, not only giving the river its name but also giving Yonkers its name, and that this section of the river had been covered with the development of the city. A year and a half ago they had broken ground on the project to uncover the flume between Broadway and the Hudson River, and the former plaza, which had served as a parking lot, had been a mess since then. But now she could see the open water flowing toward the Hudson, and her spirits were raised a little by the sight.

She found a parking place on Riverdale between Main and Hudson streets, and she fed the meter with quarters until it stopped at two hours. If that wasn't enough time, she could always come back and feed it again.

She found the building just ahead, a four-story brick structure that looked as if it dated back to the early twentieth century. It had a security system, and in order to enter she pressed the button with the number Jeanne had given her, but it didn't have an elevator, despite being in the city where the elevator was invented, so she had to climb the foot-worn stairs to the second floor. Inside the office, which seemed to occupy the entire floor, she was greeted by a young woman who could have been a student at St. Catherine, and within a few minutes a trim woman in a light blue top and khaki slacks emerged from the office behind the receptionist. She had short dark hair and brown eyes that were roiled with green.

"Carol?" the woman said, approaching her with an empathetic smile. "I'm Jeanne."

"I'm glad to meet you," Carol said, shaking hands. She figured that this woman was only around thirty since she had no wrinkles in her face. And she didn't wear a wedding ring.

"Come in," Jeanne said. "Would you like some coffee?"

"No, thanks." She followed Jeanne into an office that was large enough to accommodate a desk, a conference table, and an informal sitting area with office chairs around a glass coffee table. The furniture looked inexpensive and could have been acquired from a failed startup. The view through the wood-framed windows wasn't of the river but of the buildings on the other side of Riverdale Avenue.

"I'm sorry you had to climb the stairs," Jeanne said as they sat down in two of the office chairs, "but it keeps the rent down."

"No problem," Carol said. "And being in Yonkers must keep the rent down."

"It does," Jeanne said. "We couldn't afford to be in the city. But this location is perfect for us. I can walk to the train station in five minutes and be in the city in twenty-five minutes. I can drive to the White Plains airport in twenty minutes and fly to Washington in an hour. And I can drive to Albany in an hour and a half."

From these accounts of travel time, it was clear that Jeanne was a busy woman, yet she didn't seem in a hurry to get down to business. That, together with her accent, suggested that she wasn't from New York. "Do you rent the whole floor?"

"Yah, and the whole floor above us. I'll give you a tour, but first I'll tell you what we do," Jeanne said, shifting into the mode that Carol used in talking with prospective donors. "We're a non-governmental organization, founded eight years ago to serve the metro area. Our mission is to stop human trafficking and to help its victims. We identify victims, liberate them, and offer them appropriate services, which include shelter, counseling, therapy, skills workshops, GED classes, and job training. Our goal is to enable victims to recover from their experience and to lead productive lives. We identify traffickers, report them to law enforcement agencies, and help bring them to justice. We train police to treat victims with sensitivity and compassion, not to treat them as criminals as they did in the past and still do in many situations. We lobby for changes in the law to help victims and deter traffickers. And we raise public awareness of the problem of human trafficking."

"That sounds like a lot."

"Well, we don't work alone," Jeanne said. "We partner with other organizations that have the same mission. One of them is Polaris Project, which is based in Washington and has an office in New Jersey. Polaris was my inspiration."

"Were you involved in founding this organization?"

"Oh, yah. In case you haven't noticed from the way I talk, I'm not from New York. I'm from Milwaukee, and I went to the University of Wisconsin. I was planning to be a high school teacher, and I came to New York in a program that prepares people for teaching in inner city schools. The program's called Teach for America."

"Our college participates in that program."

"Oh, I meant to ask— Do you know Stephen Wyatt?"

"I took his course in international business twenty years ago, and I still see him on the campus."

"Then you know he runs a community center in the Bronx with his wife Marja."

"I know Marja. She's from Yonkers like I am."

"And she's Polish like I am."

With that exchange they had a bond between them.

"Well, I was in my first semester of a master's program at City College," Jeanne continued, "when I heard a woman talk about human trafficking. She mentioned Polaris Project and how it was founded by two college students, and I already knew that Teach for America was founded by a college student, so I figured that if they could do it, a Polish girl from Milwaukee could do it. So I transferred to the program in social work at Hunter College, and while I was working on my master's degree I laid the foundations for this organization. Marja was the one who suggested renting space in Yonkers."

"She's a good person. She sends a lot of students to us from the Bronx."

"I've told you what we do," Jeanne said after a pause. "Now tell me why you came to us."

"I came to you for help in finding my daughter."

"How long has she been missing?"

"Sixteen days." She didn't have to count.

"Do you have a picture of her?"

"Yeah." She got out her phone and found a picture she had taken of Amanda before their trip and handed the phone to Jeanne.

"She's a cute girl," Jeanne said, looking compassionately at the picture. "How old is she?"

"She just turned twelve in February."

Jeanne handed the phone back to her, saying: "Tell me what happened."

Carol related what had happened from the time when the girls went missing on St. Anselm to the time when the Walkers told them what they had learned from Stacy. "Until then I was still hoping they were kidnapped for ransom, but at that point I knew it was for another purpose."

"I hate to say it," Jeanne said, "but it sounds like they were trafficked for commercial sex. It fits the pattern. I mean, for girls who get kidnapped."

"How else do they get into it?"

"They get lured into it. That's how most of them get into it. But girls get kidnapped every day, and unless they're white you never hear about it."

Carol continued, relating how Stacy was going to talk with the FBI and give them the information they needed to arrest the Russians and find out where they took Amanda. "But her parents were threatened by the kidnappers, so they're afraid to let her talk with the FBI."

Jeanne nodded as if she recognized the situation. "That's what makes it so hard to stop them. People are afraid to help the police arrest them."

"Who are they?"

"They're members of global organizations. And they use the weapon of terror. They use it to keep their victims enslaved, and they use it to stop people from testifying against them."

"If they use the weapon of terror," Carol said, "doesn't that make them terrorists?"

"It does. And while the politicians wage their so-called war on terror," Jeanne said with passion, "they allow these terrorists to traffic children."

"How many children are you talking about?"

"It's hard to get a reliable number, but we estimate that more than a million children are trafficked into sex slavery every year. And I mean children."

"My daughter's age?"

"Your daughter's age. And even younger."

"That makes me sick," Carol said.

"It makes anyone with a heart sick. But the politicians allow it to happen. Some of them even benefit from it."

"How do they benefit from it?"

"They get money from these organizations. A lot of money."

Carol didn't want to believe that, but it made sense.

"So let's get back to the kidnapping," Jeanne said, refocusing.

127

"The girls were taken to Panama, where the traffickers kept them in a hotel while they fabricated passports for them, intending to fly them out of Panama."

"Where would they fly them?"

"To Europe or Asia, where people have money."

"Not to America?"

"Possibly, but not likely. The girls would have a better chance of escaping here. They'd feel lost in a foreign country."

"That still leaves a lot of countries where they could have flown Amanda to."

"It does," Jeanne said, "but my instinct and my experience tell me they probably flew her to Asia."

"Why Asia?"

Jeanne hesitated. "I'm sorry, but I have to say it like it is. Your daughter has red hair, and that would make her special in Asia."

"You mean worth more money?"

"That's right. So I think we should look for her in Japan."

"Do you have the ability to look for her there?"

"We don't have an office there," Jeanne said, "but Polaris does. We can contact them."

"What would they do?"

"They'd look for a red-haired girl at every place where sex is sold and at every place where she might be living. There's not much racial diversity in Japan, so a white girl with red hair would be noticed."

"What if they dyed her hair?"

"They wouldn't. It would lower her value."

"I just can't believe that anyone would think that way."

"You better believe it. That's how they think."

Carol closed her eyes and took a long deep breath, trying to adjust to the world that Jeanne was showing her. "Okay. What information do you need from me?"

"I have a form that you can fill out. You can do it at the table. And I also need pictures of your daughter."

"I can email you pictures from my phone."

"Good. It's better for us to have them in digital format. I'll give you an address where you can send them."

Jeanne gave her the form and the email address, and then she excused herself for a moment, leaving the office.

Carol sat down at the conference table and spent the next half hour filling out the form.

When she was done she emailed some pictures of Amanda to the address Jeanne had given her.

"Are you done?" Jeanne asked, returning to the office.

"I think so," Carol said. She handed the form to Jeanne, who stood by the table.

"It looks like you covered everything."

"And I emailed the pictures."

"Then we're ready to go. Come on," Jeanne said, already on her way out of the office.

Carol followed her.

As they went through the reception area a young woman approached Jeanne and said: "We're all set for this Thursday. We'll have a good turnout."

"Great. Thanks." When the woman had left them Jeanne said: "She was talking about our action against Village Voice Media."

"You mean the company that publishes *The Village Voice?*"

"Yah. They also publish Backpage.com which runs ads for commercial sex, including ads for underage boys and girls who are being sold like chattel. They run more than five million ads a year in this section. Can you imagine?"

"When I lived in the city I used to read the *Voice*. I thought it was a good paper."

"It was," Jeanne said. "But now they're into making money from the sex industry."

A few steps down the hall they went into an office where a young woman with her hair tied back in a pony tail was sitting at a laptop.

"This is Sonia," Jeanne said, introducing the young woman. "She works on special cases and coordinates with other organizations. Sonia, this is Carol."

"I'm glad to meet you," Sonia said, extending her hand over

the computer. She had high cheekbones and friendly dark eyes.

"Sonia went to St. Catherine."

"I went there too," Carol said. "I majored in marketing."

"When did you graduate?" Sonia asked.

"Twenty years ago. I was in the class of 1992."

"I was in the class of 2004. I majored in social work, so we wouldn't have had the same professors. But you must have had Sister Maura for religion."

"I did," Carol said. "And I just saw her. She referred me to your organization."

"Carol's daughter was kidnapped," Jeanne said.

"I'm sorry," Sonia said with feeling.

"Here's the information," Jeanne said, handing her the folder. "We're putting a top priority on this case, so please contact Polaris immediately. And contact other organizations that you think can help us. We want to find this girl as soon as possible."

"Do we have pictures of her?" Sonia asked after scanning the contents of the folder.

"Carol sent them to you," Jeanne told her.

Sonia checked her computer. "Oh, yeah. I have them. *Dios mío, ella se va tan joven.*"

"It makes you want to kill someone."

"Okay. I'm on it," Sonia said, her fingers already flying over the keys of her computer.

They continued down the hall and went into a room that was equipped as a call center. There were five stations, three of them occupied by women in casual dress. They were all talking, one of them in Spanish.

"This is our hotline," Jeanne explained. "They take inbound calls from victims and people who report suspected trafficking. They also make outbound calls to police and service providers. So they could spend an hour at a time on a single case."

"How do people learn about your hotline?"

"Mostly by word of mouth. We have people in the field who pass out information. And we do spots on television. They run late at night and early in the morning when the girls are off. They don't cost as much at those hours, and we get some stations to donate time."

"When a victim calls for help, what do you advise her to do?"

"It depends on the situation," Jeanne said. "If she's being held captive we might advise her to escape, or if she's on the street we might advise her to go to a shelter."

"Do you involve the police?"

"Yah. We work with them closely. We offer them training, and we respond to their calls when they have girls in custody. We also help them arrest traffickers."

They moved down the hall to the next room. Jeanne opened the door just long enough so that Carol could look in and see a group of girls in a circle of chairs with a counselor. After closing the door, Jeanne said: "Those girls were victims of trafficking. We provide them with individual and group counseling."

"For how long?"

"For as long as they need it. In some cases that can be a long time. At least some of them have mental disorders before they're trafficked, and those problems are aggravated by their being enslaved and sold for sex. When they come to us many of them are suffering from post-traumatic stress disorder."

"Like the troops who served in Iraq or Afghanistan?"

"Yah. They have a lot in common."

As they continued down the hall Carol asked: "Where do you get the counselors?"

"We have a full-time employee whose job is to recruit and manage the counselors. They're all licensed therapists or social workers. They work as volunteers."

"Do *you* do counseling?"

Jeanne laughed. "How did you guess? I do enough counseling to compensate for being an administrator."

"I know what you mean. For me it's more satisfying to do something than to manage other people doing it."

"There are people who like being administrators. I just don't happen to be one of them."

The next door led to a classroom, where there were several

131

girls and one boy learning how to use computers from a man with a beard.

"How's it going?" Jeanne asked him.

"Fine," he said. "These are bright kids."

After leaving the room Jeanne said: "We teach the kids practical skills, and we help them get their GEDs. Almost none of them have graduated from high school."

"How do they get lured into it?" Carol asked, unable to get that out of her mind.

"They're unhappy at home," Jeanne said. "They're living with a single mother whose boyfriend hits on them or beats them. They're doing poorly at school. And a nice man offers them a better life, with a good job and money to buy whatever they want and all the love they never got. It's hard to resist, so they go with him. Of course he turns out to be a pimp, and once he has them he doesn't let them go. If they don't do what he wants, he beats them or tortures them or threatens to kill them. He scares them shitless, so they do what he wants."

"When I saw them on the street," Carol admitted. "I thought they were prostitutes. I never realized they were slaves."

"Most people don't realize they're slaves, so we have to raise their awareness of the issue."

By now they had reached the end of the hall, and Carol asked: "What's upstairs?"

"Our shelter's upstairs. It can accommodate up to twenty victims. It has a kitchen, and a living room, and ten bedrooms. It took a little politicking to get a permit from the city," Jeanne added. "But we finally got it."

"That's part of your job too."

"Politicking? Oh, yah. I learned how to do that in Milwaukee, and Yonkers is similar. In fact, the two towns have a lot in common. They're old industrial towns on the water, they've lost their jobs in manufacturing, they're not far from a major city, they're ethnically diverse, and last but not least, they both have sizable Polish communities."

"Did you have a St. Casimir church in Milwaukee?"

"Every Polish community has a St. Casimir church. My family went to St. Casimir there, and whenever I feel homesick for a mass in Polish, I go to St. Casimir here."

"I grew up with people who went there."

"Then you know where I'm coming from."

"Well, I appreciate the time you're giving me," Carol said, "but I know you have a lot of other things to do. So tell me how I can give you a donation."

"Don't worry about that now. But maybe later you could help us with our fund raising."

"I'd be happy to do that as a volunteer."

"We can talk about it later," Jeanne said. "In the meantime you can do something to help us find your daughter."

"What? Tell me."

"You can talk with a guy who's good at finding missing girls."

"Is he a private detective?"

"Yah. But he's more than that. He's an interesting guy. He made a lot of money designing computer security systems, so he doesn't have to work for a living, and about five years ago he committed himself to our mission."

"Was there a particular reason why?"

"He told me one night over drinks. He's from Croatia, and during the war that broke up Yugoslavia his sister was taken and made a sex slave. She was thirteen, and he was eleven. When the war ended they found her remains in a military camp. Among other things the medical examiner determined that at one time or another almost all her fingers had been broken."

"Oh, my God."

"It troubled him that he was too young to do anything for his sister. But now he's in his early thirties, and he's in a position to do something for other girls. So finding them and rescuing them is a way of redeeming himself."

"How do I contact him?"

"I'll give you his card," Jeanne said, "and I'll tell him you'll be contacting him."

They went back to Jeanne's office, where she opened the top

drawer of her desk and found a card, which she handed to Carol.

The name on the card was "Saša Carević," which Carol didn't even try to pronounce.

"Sasha Cahrehvitch," Jeanne said helpfully.

"Okay. I'll call him. And thanks for everything."

"Don't thank me until we get results."

From her heart Carol said: "I can thank you already for what you're doing for those children. A month ago I wouldn't have thought but for the grace of God they could be my daughter. But now I know they *could* be my daughter, and the world will never look the same again."

Jeanne nodded as if she understood, and then she said: "We're going to find your daughter."

NINE

IT WAS AFTER eleven when Carol got to work, and she spent the next half hour reviewing the status of projects with Griselda. Everything was in place, so she took a few minutes to call the number of Saša Carević and make an appointment with him the next morning. Then she called Sister Maura to thank her for recommending Jeanne.

"I'm glad you like her," Sister Maura said. "While I have you on the phone, I have for you the phone number and the address of a lost alumna."

"How do you find them?" Carol asked.

"I don't find them. They find me."

Of course Sister Maura was being modest, as she was about all matters except baseball and politics, on which she had strong opinions. If the lost alumnae found her, it was because she put herself out there for them.

It made Carol wonder if there was anything more she could do to put herself out there for Amanda. Maybe she could talk with Lindsey about ways to keep the story alive.

For lunch she got a salad from the cafeteria and brought it back to her office. While she was eating, Tom dropped by.

"How are things going?" he asked her.

"Fine. We have everything in place for the dinner."

"I wasn't asking about the dinner."

"I know you weren't." She paused. "This morning I had a meeting with a woman whose organization rescues victims of human trafficking."

Tom grimaced. "Is that what you think happened to your daughter?"

135

"That's what the woman thinks."

"I'm sorry. Tell me how I can help you."

"You can let me take off tomorrow morning."

"Take as much time as you want," Tom said with an open gesture that supported his words. "You can take a leave of absence."

"I don't think I need one, but if I do I'll let you know."

Tom lingered. "So is this organization going to help you find your daughter?"

"They're going to try. They work with other organizations that have the same mission, so they have resources."

"Is human trafficking a major problem?"

"Yah," she said, sounding like Jeanne. "More than a million children are trafficked into sex slavery every year."

"If that's the case, then we should be fighting the human traffickers instead of the drug traffickers."

"From what I've heard, the same people are involved in both activities."

"Well, I don't care about the drugs."

"I don't either." But the mention of drugs made her wonder if Amanda's captors would use drugs to control her. "Anyway, I like this organization."

"Are they in the city?"

"No. They're in Yonkers."

"Well, maybe we should do something with them."

"You mean to promote awareness of human trafficking?"

"Yeah. It would be good for them and good for the college. After all," Tom added, "more than seventy percent of our students are women."

"We have an alumna working for them," Carol said. "Her name is Sonia. I don't know her last name, but I can get it. She was class of 2004."

"Why don't you have Griselda contact her."

"Good idea. They're both Latinas."

Around three she texted Matthew asking where he was, and within about five minutes he responded saying he was at Jeff's house. She wondered if her regular checking might have some kind of negative effect on him, and she decided it would be better for him to text her after school to let her know where he was going. If he forgot to do that, she could always text him, but one way or another she had to know where he was.

Of course her mother hadn't always known where she was at that age, and they had lived in a neighborhood where a lot more could happen to children. Maybe, as her mother had suggested, by trying to protect her children she was making them more vulnerable.

Luckily, she had work that interrupted these thoughts.

While she was making dinner that evening, with Matthew in his room, she told Brian about her meeting with Jeanne. He sat at the table, sipping a beer and listening. He let her talk without asking any questions until she got to the point where Jeanne concluded that the girls had been trafficked for commercial sex, not kidnapped for ransom.

"So we're going to assume that Amanda was trafficked?" he asked with his voice cracking.

"I think we should. We've been hoping and praying she wasn't, but I think we have to face reality. Our hoping and praying won't help her."

"Praying is supposed to help her," he said, staring into the beer bottle.

"I know," Carol said, "but even Sister Maura doesn't wait for God to do something."

"We haven't been waiting for God to do something."

"I didn't say we have been. But I feel like we have to do more. If Amanda was trafficked, we don't have much time to stop them from hurting her."

"Oh, God," Brian said with tears forming in his troubled eyes. "I just can't bear to think about it."

She went to him.

"Our poor little girl," he cried in anguish, putting his arms around her hips and pressing his face against her apron.

"We're going to find her," she said, believing it.

"I don't know how," he said in despair.

"We have an appointment tomorrow with a guy who's good at finding missing girls."

He withdrew his head from her apron and looked up at her. "Who recommended him?"

"Jeanne did."

"Is he in the city?"

"He's on Cabrini Boulevard."

He wiped his eyes with the back of his hand and said: "I'll do a search on the address so we know how to get there."

During dinner Matthew told them a boy at school had teased him about his sister, saying she hadn't been kidnapped, she had run away. He didn't know where the boy had gotten that idea, but Carol knew how kids repeated things they heard from their parents, so she concluded that the boy had heard his parents say it. But she didn't ask Matthew for the boy's name since she didn't want to know which neighbor or friend was saying such things behind her back. She hoped it wasn't someone who expressed sympathy to her face.

Later, as she and Brian were in bed watching Channel 12 News, she remembered her intention to keep the story alive. There was nothing about the missing girls, and she didn't expect them to report that there was nothing to report. So after they shut off the television and turned off the lights, she lay back and wondered what information she could give Lindsey that would prompt the station to run an update of the story.

The next morning they drove to the city in Brian's car since it was behind her car in their driveway. They headed south on the Saw Mill Parkway, crossed over the Henry Hudson Bridge, and took the exit for the George Washington Bridge, but instead of going to the bridge they doubled back and headed north on Riverside Drive. They turned onto 181st Street and then left onto Cabrini Boulevard. They found the parking garage that Saša had advised her to use, and they left the car there and walked north on Cabrini. The building, which was just up the street, looked as if it dated before World War II and was about fifteen stories high. It had a security system, and Carol pressed the number Saša had given her.

Saša lived on the top floor, and he was standing in the open door of his apartment waiting for them. Short and pudgy, with spiky light hair, wild blue eyes, and pink cheeks, he reminded her of a creature in a movie from the *Lord of the Rings* series, which she had rented for the kids. He certainly didn't fit her image of a private detective.

"I'm Saša," he said with a foreign accent. "I assume you're Carol and Brian Delaney."

"Yeah. I'm glad to meet you," she said.

They completed the introductions, and then they went into his apartment. To the right was a small kitchen, and ahead was a spacious living room with high-tech furniture and a large window that offered a view of the Hudson and the greening Palisades across the river.

"You have a spectacular view," she said, admiring it.

"That's the main attraction," Saša said. "But I also like the location. I'm in the city, but I'm also in a neighborhood. Would you like some coffee?"

"No, thanks. But I'd like some water."

"I have good water. I'll get some for you." He went into the kitchen, and after a few minutes he emerged with a filled pitcher in one hand and three glasses dangling from the other. "This isn't from a plastic bottle, it's filtered from the tap."

"We drink that too. I don't like the taste of chlorine."

"Chlorine not only tastes bad, it's bad for you. If it kills living things in the water, what do you think it does to us?"

He led them toward the window and set the pitcher and the glasses on a coffee table, which had a black top and chrome legs. He invited them to sit down in chairs that matched the coffee table, and he poured water into the glasses. He took a sip as if he was tasting wine, and then he nodded as if the water was all right to drink. He sat down opposite them, slipping out of his flip-

139

flops and drawing his legs up under him, sitting like a Buddha. "Jeanne told me what happened to your daughter, so you don't have to repeat the whole story. But I need to talk with the police detective on St. Anselm. Could you give me his name and his phone number?"

"It's Detective Inspector Ramsey," Carol said.

"Do you know his first name?"

She looked at Brian, who shook his head. "No. We don't. But we have his phone number."

Saša waited while she took out her phone and found Ramsey in her directory and read out the number.

"Is that a cell phone?"

"Yes," she said.

"Good. I don't want to use their land line." Saša entered the number into his phone, and then he said. "Now, let's talk about the girl who escaped. How did that happen?"

"She told her parents the Russians had brought them new clothes and new passports, and they were leaving the hotel when the deskman yelled after them. They both turned around, which gave the girls an opportunity to run away."

"They must have forgotten to do something."

"Like pay the bill," Brian muttered.

"Whatever the reason," Carol said, "the girls took advantage of the opportunity. There were people on the street, so the men couldn't shoot them."

"When did you hear about it?" Saša asked.

She thought for a moment. "Frank called us on Thursday as I was about to leave for work."

"What time did he call you?"

"Around eight thirty."

"Now, let's follow the sequence of events," Saša said as if he was reading from a power point. "The Russians checked out of the hotel to take the girls to the airport. They were distracted by the deskman. The girls ran away. One girl escaped. She found the police, the police called her parents, her father called Frank, and Frank called you. So it happened on Thursday."

"How do you figure?' Brian asked.

"If it happened on Wednesday," Saša explained, "you would have heard about it sooner. Now, people check out of hotels in the morning, and we're on daylight savings time and Panama isn't, and it probably took about three hours from the time the Russians checked out of the hotel to the time Frank called you. So it happened around five thirty in the morning."

"Would there have been people on the street at that time?"

"Oh, yes. In tropical countries a lot of people start work early, before it gets too hot. So they would have been on their way to work at that time."

"If they were taking the girls to the airport," Carol said, "they must have had a morning flight."

"They must have," Saša said. "Now, it takes about a half hour to get to the airport from Panama City. So they were on a flight that departed between seven and eight in the morning."

"Wouldn't they have had to be at the airport two hours before departure time?"

"An hour before departure time would have been enough. They wouldn't have wanted the girls at the airport any longer than necessary. They would have been too visible there."

"Well, how would they have stopped the girls from escaping at the airport?"

"By telling them that if they escaped," Saša said grimly, "their families would be killed."

"But that didn't stop the girls from trying to escape in front of the hotel," Brian pointed out.

"They saw a chance to escape, and they were probably so excited they didn't think about their families."

"So you'll get a list of flights that departed from Panama last Thursday between seven and eight in the morning."

"That's right, though I'll make the interval a little wider so I don't miss a possible flight."

"But how will you know what flight she was on? The airlines don't give out that information."

Saša smiled. "I have a lot of experience in computer security,

141

and if you understand these systems you can always find a way into them."

"I assume she wasn't traveling alone," Carol said.

"She would have had a guardian—someone to remind her that if she tried to escape, her family would be killed."

"Then you'll look in the system for a man traveling with a girl?" Brian asked.

"I'll look for a man traveling with his daughter," Saša said. "That wouldn't raise so many questions."

"Stacy told her parents she had a Russian name on her fake passport," Carol said.

"So I'll look for a Russian traveling with his daughter."

"What if the flight wasn't direct?"

"Then I'll have to find the connecting flight. But that won't be a problem." Saša waited as if to let them ask more questions, and then he said: "Now, I want to know more about the threat the Walkers received. When did it happen?"

"On Sunday night," Brian said. "They got a phone call, which Stacy's mother answered. A man told her that if Stacy talked with anyone outside her family, they would not only kill Stacy but they would also kill her sister. And they would kill them in a way that made them suffer as much as possible."

"That sounds like the Russians I know," Saša said wryly. "Did the Walkers get the call on their land line?"

"I think they did," Carol said. "They implied that either of them could have answered it."

"Did they say what time it was?"

"No, they only said it was Sunday night. But they didn't say it woke them up, so it must have been before they went to bed."

"Do you know what time they go to bed?"

"I think they go to bed by eleven. Richard has to get up early to catch a train to the city."

"Then we'll assume they received the call between six and eleven. That's a reasonably short interval."

"Can you trace that phone call?" Brian asked.

"Oh, yes. We do it all the time."

"If Richard had told Frank about the phone call, could he have traced it?"

"Yes. He could have. And within a few hours he would have known where it came from."

"So who's going to trace it? You or Frank?"

"I can do it faster. Frank would have to go through a process."

"Then go ahead," Carol said. "What do you need?"

"I need the Walkers' phone number."

Knowing it by heart, she gave it to him.

"What if the caller used a payphone?" Brian asked.

"I could still trace it," Saša said, "though it wouldn't lead me to the caller. But I don't think he used a payphone. There aren't many payphones left, and they're in public places where he could have been observed. So I think he used a cell phone with a prepaid card."

"With a prepaid card he could hide his identity, couldn't he?"

"Yes. But he couldn't hide the phone. And if I can find the phone, I can find him."

"Should we pay you something now?" Carol asked.

Saša shook his head. "I don't charge for my services. But when I find your daughter, you can make a donation to Jeanne's organization."

"We intend to do that anyway, but—"

Saša raised his hand to silence her, saying: "I don't do this for money. Did Jeanne explain?"

"She did," Carol told him, sensing that he didn't want to talk about it. "Well, if you need to reach us, you can call me on my cell phone."

"Okay," Saša said, looking eager to get started.

He accompanied them to the door, and after shaking his hand they left the apartment. They didn't talk until they were in the elevator, and then Brian asked: "What do you think?"

"I think he can help us find Amanda."

"When you asked about paying him something, I noticed he said *when* he found our daughter we could make a donation. He didn't say *if* he found her."

"Jeanne said he's good at finding missing girls."

They left the building and walked to the garage, where they paid for parking and waited while an attendant fetched the car.

"I've been wanting to call Lindsey," Carol said, "and tell her something that would keep the story alive. And I finally thought of something."

"Tell me in the car," Brian said.

Not wanting to distract him, she waited until they were on the Henry Hudson Parkway, and then she said: "It bothers me that we're losing time because the Walkers won't let their daughter talk with Frank."

"It bothers me too," Brian said. "And we lost two days because Richard didn't tell him about the phone call."

"Even if Richard *had* told him about the phone call, we still would have lost time because the Walkers wouldn't let their daughter talk with Frank."

"I wonder why he didn't tell Frank about the phone call."

"Maybe he didn't want to admit that he was afraid."

"But he admitted it to us."

"Well, maybe he cares more about what Frank thinks of him."

"Maybe. His relationship with Frank is professional, while his relationship with us is only personal."

Pursuing her idea, Carol said: "So I thought of telling Lindsey that the Walkers wouldn't let their daughter give information to the FBI that would have enabled them to find Amanda."

"What would that accomplish?"

"It would put pressure on the Walkers."

"Pressure to do what?"

"To let their daughter talk with Frank, so he could get what Ramsey needs to arrest the Russians."

Brian held the wheel steady as a low black car roared by them going at least seventy. With the curves ahead, it would have to slow down or else have an accident. "Well, now that we have Saša helping us, he could get what Ramsey needs."

"I have confidence in Saša, but I want him to have Frank's support."

"From the way he talked," Brian said, "I got the feeling he's worked on these cases with Frank before. So he just has to contact Frank if he needs support."

She stewed for a while, and then she said: "It still bothers me that we're losing time because the Walkers won't let their daughter talk with Frank."

"What do you think we would have done in their position?"

"I think we would have let Amanda talk with Frank."

"Are you sure we would have?"

"I'm pretty sure. I'd have known what would happen to their daughter if the police didn't find her quickly. And that if I didn't help them, I couldn't live with myself."

"You'd have risked the lives of *our* children?"

"I'm pretty sure I would have, based on what I know now."

"What do you know now that you didn't know before?"

It came right out. "I know that the lives of our children are always at risk, so it's a delusion to think we can protect them."

Brian reflected, keeping his eyes on the road ahead of them. "I've reached the same conclusion. I've been thinking about how the resort has a gate to protect the guests. But the people inside have no idea what it's like outside."

"Our children had no idea. That's a difference between them and us. At their age we knew what it was like outside."

"Of course we're responsible for their having no idea."

"You don't have to tell me," Carol said, aware of a sore spot. "My mother already told me."

"So now we know we can't protect them. And we're pretty sure that if we'd been in the Walkers' position, we would have let Amanda talk with Frank."

"With bodyguards."

He slowed as they approached the toll station. Since they had an E-ZPass device on the windshield, the toll would be paid automatically so he didn't have to fumble around for coins. "I think bodyguards are like gates. They give people a false sense of security."

"Couldn't they stop a professional hit man?"

"I don't know," Brian said. "But remember what we told the Walkers. We told them that if the kidnappers were caught, they wouldn't have a reason for carrying out their threat."

"They could want revenge."

"If they were charged with kidnapping, then getting revenge wouldn't help their case."

"You make them sound rational."

"They *are* rational. Nothing could be more rational than doing the things they do for money."

"You mean they're pure business people."

"They have to be. If they cared about anything except money, they wouldn't be involved in human trafficking."

As they accelerated, leaving the toll station behind them, Carol persisted. "So why shouldn't we put pressure on the Walkers to let their daughter talk with Frank?"

"I don't know. I think we'll hear from Saša before they let her talk with Frank."

"Maybe we will. But how long should we give Saša?"

"Before we put pressure on the Walkers?"

"Yeah. It could take them a while to respond to the pressure."

After a silence Brian asked: "Have you thought about how the Walkers would feel if everyone knew they weren't willing to help us find our daughter?"

"I've tried not to think about that."

"If it was our only option, I wouldn't give a rat's ass how the Walkers felt. But it's not our only option, and at this point I don't think it would help us find Amanda sooner."

"Maybe it wouldn't," Carol admitted. "But it's still an option. So how long should we give Saša?"

"Since he said it was easy to trace a call, I think we should give him until tomorrow."

"Okay. And I hope we don't have to put pressure on the Walkers. I mean, I *have* thought about how they'd feel if everyone knew they weren't willing to help us, and I wouldn't want to be in that position."

"They probably feel bad about not helping us."

"I'm sure Donna does, but I don't know about Richard."

"If she feels bad about it, then he does too."

"You think she influences how he feels?"

"You influence how I feel," Brian said, glancing at her. "Why should they be any different?"

She gave him a friendly punch on the arm to let him know she felt they had resolved the issue in a satisfactory manner.

Instead of going home and then driving back to the college, she had Brian drop her off there on the way to Hastings, and she arrived in time for a working lunch in the conference room to review the status of events. She was able to keep her mind on the discussion enough so she wasn't free riding, but she wasn't fully concentrating. She kept seeing her daughter on a plane with a "guardian" next to her, ready to remind her that if she tried to escape they would kill her family. Trying to imagine what her daughter was feeling, she remembered when a gang of boys attacked her and a friend in Tibbetts Park—at the time she was a year older than Amanda. Though they were rescued by a police officer with no damage done, it was a terrifying experience, but it was nothing like what might be happening to Amanda.

Unable to wait for a report from Saša, she decided to call Donna and plead with her to let Stacy talk with Frank, and back in her office she punched the number of Donna's cell phone. She only got Donna's voicemail, and she left a message saying: "Please help us. You know what they're doing to Amanda."

Sitting at her desk, she wondered if she and Brian had made the right decision about the Walkers. Maybe they shouldn't wait another day to put pressure on them. Maybe she should call Lindsey now and give her an update on the story.

But what if she and Brian *had* been in the Walkers' position? They were pretty sure they would have let Amanda talk with

Frank, but would they have really let her? She could imagine what it was like being in the Walker's position, but she didn't know what it was like. And though she was pretty sure about it, she didn't know if she would have risked the lives of both her children to help find another woman's child. In fact, the more she thought about it, the more she understood why Donna wouldn't let her daughter talk with Frank: when facing a threat, a mother had to save her own children.

She left her office in time to catch the five-twenty bus. Though she didn't use the bus often, she kept a schedule in her office so she would have the information in case she needed it.

As she approached Broadway, she saw a group of students waiting for a south-bound bus, most of them with backpacks. Since she was going in the other direction, she crossed the street and waited at the bus stop there.

The bus arrived on time, and she boarded it, taking a seat in the middle by the window. Within a few minutes of getting under way the bus stopped at the hospital, where some people got off—they were probably visitors since they weren't in scrubs and they looked like they were coming from work.

As the bus moved forward Carol reflected on the fact that when she was Amanda's age her family didn't have a car, so if she had to go anywhere beyond walking distance she took the bus. She took the bus to school, going north on Broadway and getting off at Shonnard and walking over to Sacred Heart, and she took the bus home. She didn't go anywhere in a car until she reached driving age, when a few of her friends had access to a family car. And even then she still depended mainly on the bus.

Maybe if instead of being driven everywhere by car Amanda had learned to use the bus system, she would have known more about the real world. At least she would have been exposed to different people.

Carol got off at Hastings and crossed the street to buy food at Hastings Prime Meats, which was owned and managed by Koreans. It not only had meat, chicken, and fish but it also had fresh produce, dairy products, bread, and other things, including some prepared dinners. Since it was a short walk from her house, she shopped there often.

She was standing in front of the meat counter wondering what to buy for dinner when her phone vibrated.

Taking it out of her handbag, she saw from the identification that it was Saša.

"Hello?" she said anxiously.

"We traced the phone call," he told her.

"You did?" Her heart was already pounding.

"And guess what. They used a phone that belongs to Stacy Walker."

"What? Can I call you right back? I'm in a public place."

"Okay. But we have to decide how to move on this."

"I understand. I'll call you right back."

TEN

CAROL LEFT THROUGH the back door, which led to a parking lot—it had a magnificent view of the Hudson that was graced by the silhouette of the water tank from the dismantled plant of the Anaconda Wire & Cable Company. The sun was setting over the Palisades, and the sky was reddening.

She went down the steps and crossed the lot and stopped in a space between two cars and called Saša back, her mind already evaluating possible courses of action based on his discovery. By the time he was on the phone again she had already decided on the course that would produce the quickest results.

"Have you told anyone else about this?" she asked him.

"No. I wanted to get your input," he said. "Now, this is what I think happened. They took the phone from the girl and kept it. The police didn't find it on the yacht because one of them had it on him. It came in handy when they decided to threaten the Walkers. They were confident that the Walkers would never tell anyone about the phone call, so no one would trace it."

"If Richard hadn't told us about the phone call, we wouldn't have known about it."

"Then it's lucky he told you. And I think the Russians still believe that no one but the Walkers knows about the call, so they might still have the phone."

"If they do still have it, then we can catch them with it."

"They were on St. Anselm when they made the call, and they may still be there."

"Ramsey will know if they're still there."

"I think that instead of going through Frank, we should talk directly with Ramsey."

This was what she had decided.

"Frank would have to go through a process," Saša explained. "He would have to tell the government of St. Anselm that he was involved in an investigation on their territory. And I don't think we can trust them."

"Ramsey doesn't trust them."

"I know he doesn't. I talked with him this morning after you left, and he believes that the Russians are paying someone at a high level for their status on the island. That's how they usually operate. They use their money to buy favors."

"So we should call Ramsey and give him this information."

"Yes. We should. Where are you now?"

"I'm in a parking lot."

"Do you have any privacy?"

"Yeah," Carol said, looking around. There was no one else in the parking lot.

"Then call him now, and I'll patch into your conversation."

She ended the call, then found Ramsey in her directory and called him. He answered after two rings, and as she started talking with him she heard a tone that sounded like a participant joining a conference call.

"Who is it?" she asked cautiously.

"It's Saša," he said. "Hello, Inspector Ramsey."

"Hello," Ramsey said. "What's happening?"

"We have some information for you," Saša said exultantly. "You know the phone call the Walkers got from the kidnappers? Well, they used Stacy Walker's phone. And they made the call from St. Anselm."

"They did?" There was a long pause. "I can't believe they would do such a stupid thing."

"I can't either," Saša said. "They must have been confident that the Walkers would never tell anyone about the phone call. And of course unless we catch them with it, the phone won't implicate them."

"They're on the island now. If I can take them by surprise, I might catch them with it."

"If they had the phone a few days ago, they might still have it."

151

"They might. They act like they believe they can get away with anything on this island."

"What do you need in order to justify a search?"

"I need probable cause," Ramsey said.

"I think you have it," Saša said. "You know the phone belongs to one of the girls who was kidnapped. You know it was used to threaten her family. And you know the call was made from St. Anselm. That should be enough."

"I think it is enough. And if I go through a process someone might warn them."

"We haven't told the FBI about it. We wanted to give you a chance to act before our governments get involved."

"Then I don't have to worry about our government—unless the Russians don't have the phone. But if they don't, then I'll just have to deal with that situation."

"I believe," Saša said, "that wherever they were taking Amanda, she's already there. So the sooner you arrest them—"

"I understand," Ramsey said. "I'm on my way there."

"Thank you," Carol said, appreciating the risk he was taking.

"Don't thank me until we find your daughter."

She stayed on the line after Ramsey had hung up, and she asked Saša: "Have you made any progress in finding out where they took Amanda?"

"I have," Saša said. "I tracked a man and a girl with a Russian name from Panama to Lima. I'm trying to find out where they went from there. But if they were going to Europe, they wouldn't have gone to Lima. So they must have been going to Asia."

"Where in Asia?"

"My guess would be Japan."

"Should I give that information to Jeanne?"

"It's not information, it's only a guess. And I'll give it to her. But you might want to talk with her too." He evidently sensed her need to stay involved.

"Okay. Well, when do you think we'll hear from Ramsey?"

"We should hear from him within an hour. He'll probably call you first, so please don't get into a long phone conversation with anyone."

She smiled. "I won't."

After ending the call she turned as if to go back into Prime Meats, but she changed her mind and gave up the idea of making dinner. Instead, she would order pizza.

She walked out to Spring Street and then proceeded to Brian's office, where she found him alone at a drafting board. He looked up and smiled at her, but there was a look of despair in his eyes that pierced her heart.

"I have some good news," she told him. "Saša traced the call from the kidnappers. They used Stacy's phone."

"They did?" He banged his fist on the drafting board. "Then Ramsey can arrest them."

"He can if he catches them with the phone. He's on his way to their house now."

Brian exhaled as if he was trying to empty his lungs of a poisonous gas. "Oh, I hope to God he catches them with it."

"If he does, he still has to make them talk."

"In this situation he should be allowed to torture them."

"That's how I feel. They've tortured us."

"I'm sorry," Brian said, reaching for her hand.

"I'm sorry too," she said, taking it.

They comforted each other in silence for a while, and then he asked: "When do you think we'll hear from Ramsey?"

"Saša thinks within an hour. So let's go home and wait there."

Without touching any of his work he turned out the lights and followed her out, locking the door behind them.

As they walked along Maple Avenue they passed the houses of their neighbors, who were safe at home with their children having dinner or watching television. And she felt as if she no longer had anything in common with them, now that she had been exposed to a world where children were kidnapped and sold as slaves.

When they got home she went upstairs and checked to see if

Matthew was all right. As usual he was reclining on his bed with his computer, lost in cyberspace.

"How was school?"

"It was all right."

"Does that mean five on a scale from zero to ten?"

"Yeah. Or maybe four."

"Did anyone say anything about your sister?"

"They've stopped talking about her."

"That's good," she said. "Well, we've made some progress in finding her."

Matthew looked up as if she had caught his attention.

"This morning we hired a private detective."

"A private detective?" His eyes lit up.

"He has an idea where they took Amanda, and he's helping the police find her."

"Will I get to meet him?"

"Yeah, later. We're waiting to hear from the detective on St. Anselm. He's on his way to the kidnappers' house."

"Will he find Amanda there?"

"No. But he'll find out where she is."

"By torturing them?" Matthew asked with a look of glee.

"He can't torture them. But he can threaten them with a long jail sentence."

"Can he threaten them with a death sentence?"

"Maybe." She wondered if her son's predilection for violence was caused by the electronic games he played, or if it reflected the intensity of his love for his sister. Hoping it was simply the latter, she said: "So we won't have dinner until we hear from the police detective."

"That's okay," Matthew told her as if he wouldn't have any trouble passing the time.

"Have you done your homework?"

"Yeah. I didn't have much."

Though her memory could have been faulty, she believed that at his age she had hours of homework every day. Did she have more homework because she went to a different kind of school? Or did schools in general assign less homework? She parked these questions in the back of her mind since they weren't her highest priority now. "We're going to order pizza. Would you like yours with sausage?"

"Yes, please."

She bent over and kissed him, making sure she didn't block his view of the computer screen. "I'll let you know when the pizza arrives."

She went into the master bedroom and changed into jeans and a cotton pullover, and then she went down to the kitchen, where Brian was sitting at the table with his hands clasped in front of him as if he was praying. He had the bedroom phone on the table so he could get on the line when Ramsey called.

She got two bottles of beer out of the refrigerator, opened them, and joined him at the table. They sat in silence with only one thing on their minds and no need to talk about it.

After a while the phone rang.

It was Ramsey, who said: "We caught them. One of them had the phone in his pocket."

"Thank God," she said. "Did you arrest them?"

"We have them in custody. We questioned them, but they wouldn't tell us anything. They're waiting for their lawyer."

"Can he have them released?" Brian asked.

"No. But he can drag things out. So I was looking for a way to speed things up, and I thought of threatening them with extradition."

"How would that work?"

"Your government would ask our government to have them taken to your country, where they would be tried for kidnapping and for making a death threat. If they're convicted, they could get a life sentence."

"But wouldn't that take a long time?"

"It would," Ramsey said. "But it would take only a minute to *threaten* them with extradition."

"I thought they bought your government."

155

"They did. But with the evidence we have, our government won't refuse to cooperate with your government. And whoever they bribed already has the money in his Swiss bank account, so he doesn't care what happens to the Russians as long as they're in prison."

"So what's your next step?"

"My next step is to talk with Frank. But before taking it," Ramsey said, "I wanted to let you know we caught them."

"When will you talk with him?" Carol asked.

"Right after I hang up—if I can reach him. I don't have to work things out with him. I only have to know if the threat of extradition would be credible."

"I understand. Well, we won't delay you."

They ended the call, still sitting at the table.

"Until now I hoped we'd find her," Carol said. "I almost believed we'd find her. But now I know we're going to find her. I just don't know—"

"What damage has been done," Brian said, completing her sentence.

They reached across the table and found each other's hand.

"Did you hear from the police detective?" Matthew asked, coming into the kitchen.

"Yes. We did," Carol said. "He caught the kidnappers."

"Did they tell him where Amanda is?"

"Not yet. But they'll tell him." She believed that one way or another Ramsey would make them tell him.

She called Sam's and ordered two small pies, one with sausage and the other with garlic. As usual they told her it would be ready in about fifteen minutes.

Brian had just left in the car with Matthew to pick up the pizzas when the phone rang again.

It was Saša, who said: "We've tracked them from Lima. They were on a flight to Tokyo."

"How long ago?"

"Two days ago."

"Do you think it's their final destination?"

"I think it is. Tokyo is a big market." Saša didn't have to say for what.

"Then we should tell Jeanne. An organization she works with has an office there."

"I've already told her, and she's going to contact them. It's six in the morning in Tokyo now."

"Did Ramsey call you?"

"He didn't have to. I listened to your conversation."

"You did?" She was impressed, though her loss of privacy made her uneasy.

"I like his idea to threaten the Russians with extradition. The only thing better," Saša added, "might be to threaten to send them back to Russia, where they could spend the rest of their lives in Siberia."

"For kidnapping?"

"No. For stealing from the thugs who run that country."

"So they're looking for Amanda in Tokyo," Carol said, "and I know they'll find her. But if Ramsey could make the Russians tell him where she is—"

"It would speed things up. I don't know him that well, but I have a feeling he'll get that information out of them."

"I do too," she said, glad to have her feeling confirmed by a professional.

"The next thing that'll happen," Saša said, "is we'll hear from Ramsey or we'll hear from Jeanne. Since there's nothing more you can do right now, you should try to get some sleep. You need to rest for your trip to Tokyo."

After ending the call she remained at the table, trying to imagine what lay ahead of her. The main thing was to find her daughter and rescue her, but at that point the process of recovery would only begin. It was too soon to know what that would be like. She only knew that whatever it was like, it would be better than not finding her daughter.

That night, as if she was following Saša's advice, she slept well for the first time since the girls had gone missing.

The next morning, as she was pouring some cereal into a bowl for Matthew, the phone rang.

It was Ramsey, who said: "I have good news. They told us where your daughter is."

"Thank God. Is she in Tokyo?"

"Yes. They gave us the address, which I gave to Saša. He's working with an organization that has an office in Tokyo. They should be able to find your daughter right away."

At that moment Matthew appeared, looking half asleep.

She stretched out an arm and drew him toward her, saying: "We have good news."

"Did they find her?" he asked.

"They know where she is. I'm talking with my son," she explained to Ramsey.

"I had to negotiate with the Russians," he said. "I had to offer them something better than life in prison."

"What did you offer them?"

"Fifteen years in prison here. When they see what it's like, they may wish they'd accepted life in an American prison."

"What about the other missing girls?"

"They told me where they are, or where they were the last they knew. So we have a chance of finding them too."

"Saša can probably help you find them."

"I already have him working on it. Well, I better get off and free up your line. He may be trying to reach you now."

She wondered if he was listening to their conversation, but she didn't ask if he was there.

Meanwhile, her son had wriggled out of her hug and was eating the cereal, taking it out of the bowl with his hand as if it was peanuts.

She called the college and left a message for Tom that she wouldn't be at work that day, and then she called Brian, who had gone to his office early to catch up on his work and occupy his mind while they were waiting for further developments. She told him what Ramsey had reported, and she left it that she would call him back when she heard from Saša.

She was in the living room, wondering what chore she could do in whatever time she had before the next phone call, when her cell phone vibrated.

She assumed it was Saša, but it was Jeanne, who said: "They found your daughter."

After a sigh of relief she asked: "Where did they find her?"

"She wasn't in a good place. But she's safe now. She's with people who know how to care for victims."

"You mean she was already——?"

"Yah," Jeanne said. "She wouldn't talk with them about it, but she let a doctor examine her, so they know what happened to her physically."

"Oh, God." They hadn't found her in time.

"It's still too early for them to assess her mental condition, but at least there's one positive thing. She asked them for her mother and father."

"Wouldn't most girls do that?"

"Most girls in her situation don't want to see their mothers, who probably abused them. And most don't have fathers, except in a biological sense."

"Are you saying she's lucky?"

"I'm only saying it could be worse."

"I understand," Carol said after reflecting. "And I don't want to sound ungrateful, but——"

"You don't sound ungrateful," Jeanne said. "You sound like a concerned mother."

She called Brian and told him they had found Amanda but without mentioning what had happened to her since she would have to do that face to face. They decided she should book the next flight to Tokyo that they could get on, and he said he would be home in ten minutes.

She called the airline they usually used and booked a flight that departed at one fifteen that afternoon. Not knowing what to expect in Tokyo, she didn't book a return flight.

She called Ramsey to tell him the news. He had already heard from Saša, but he finally let her thank him.

"You're a wonderful man," she told him. "Your daughters are lucky to have you as a father."

"You should tell that to my daughters," he joked. "Maybe they'd believe it."

Then she called Saša, who said: "I'm sorry we didn't find her sooner."

"If you hadn't helped us, we might never have found her."

"Well, you should give most of the credit to Ramsey. He wouldn't tell you, but I can tell you. When he arrested the Russians they threatened to kill his daughters."

"They did?"

"It might have been an idle threat, but it didn't stop him. Ramsey risked the lives of his own daughters to find yours."

"Then I didn't thank him enough."

"You did. He doesn't want his daughters to grow up in a world where children are kidnapped and sold as slaves."

She was ending the call when Brian came into the kitchen. She went to him and hugged him, hoping to find the strength to tell him what had happened to Amanda.

"Did you get us on a flight?" he asked.

"Yeah, it's at one fifteen," she said.

"What about Matthew?"

"I'm going to ask Nancy if he can stay with them."

"That would be better than leaving him with your parents."

"Yeah, this way he can walk to school."

"I'll go upstairs and get out the suitcases."

She let him go, and taking advantage of this reprieve she called Nancy.

"Hi, Carol," Nancy said, answering.

"I hope I didn't interrupt your work," Carol said tentatively.

"You didn't interrupt my work. I'm sitting at my desk with a blank piece of paper in front of me. For some reason, I can't come up with any ideas."

"We just heard that they found Amanda."

"They found Amanda? Oh, I'm so happy for you."

"She's in Tokyo. We're flying there this afternoon, and I wondered if you could—"

"Take Matthew for a few days? I'd love to," Nancy said. "He's such a nice boy."

"Thanks. I'm going to pack a bag for him. He can stop and pick it up after school and then go to your house."

"Jeff will go with him. I'll text Jeff and let him know what's happening."

"I don't know how long we'll be gone, but it shouldn't be more than a few days."

"Stay there as long as you need to," Nancy told her.

She thanked Nancy again, and then she called her mother.

After hearing the news her mother, direct as usual, asked: "What did they do to her?"

"I don't know. I know there was some physical damage, but I don't know the extent of the mental damage."

"Well, let us know when you get home. We're here for you."

"Thanks. Can you tell me why I feel this is my fault?"

"You're her mother. Whenever anything happened to my children, I felt it was my fault."

"But it wasn't your fault."

"You're right, it wasn't. But I felt it was, so I know why you feel that way."

"How long did it take you to realize it wasn't your fault?"

"It didn't take long, but it took long to get over the feeling. And maybe I didn't get over it," her mother added. "Maybe I just learned to live with it."

After ending the call with her mother she texted Matthew telling him they had found Amanda and asking him to call her at the first opportunity. At that point, to relieve Donna of whatever guilt she might feel for not letting Stacy talk with Frank, she decided to let her know they had found Amanda. Not wanting to get into a conversation with Donna, she composed a simple text message. She was sending this message when Brian returned.

"The suitcases are in our bedroom," he told her. "I've already packed mine."

"I called Nancy, and Matthew's going to stay with them. I also called my mother," she said, delaying the inevitable. "I have to call Tom and tell him what's happening."

"Before you call him," Brian said, looking at her with apprehension, "tell me what you're keeping from me."

She hesitated. She couldn't bear what it would do to him.

"Tell me. I can take it."

She tried to find the least painful way of telling him, and finally she said: "We didn't find her in time. They'd already started her."

"How do you know?" he asked with tears of pain gathering in his eyes.

"Jeanne told me a doctor examined her."

"Oh, God," he cried, looking upward. "Why did You let this happen to her?"

She took him in her arms, saying: "She'll be all right. With our love we can heal her."

"Our poor little girl," he sobbed against her shoulder.

"With our love we can heal her," Carol repeated.

At that moment her phone rang. It was Matthew, who asked: "Where did they find her?"

"In Tokyo. We're flying there this afternoon."

"Can I go with you?"

"No, it's a long trip, and it would be boring for you."

"I could take my computer with me."

"It would still be boring. And anyway we want you to stay so you can welcome your sister home."

"Am I going to stay with grandma?"

"You're going to stay with Jeff."

"Oh, good. Does he know?"

"His mother should have told him by now."

"I'll go and find him."

"We'll be gone by the time you get home from school, but I packed a bag for you. It's in your room."

"I can walk home with Jeff, and then we can go to his place."

162

"We should be home in a few days. I'll let you know when we're coming."

"Okay."

"I love you."

"I love you too."

As she ended the call she noticed that Brian had squared his shoulders and raised his chin and stopped his tears.

"So?" she said, prompting him to speak.

"With our love we can heal her," he said as if he believed it.

She raised her hands and offered them to him, palms toward him, and he reciprocated. Their hands touched and grasped each other to seal what she felt was the most important pledge of their lives.

ELEVEN

FROM THE MOMENT they got off the plane at the Tokyo airport Carol felt she was in a different world. The airport looked like any airport, and there were the same frustrations in going through immigration, recovering luggage, and clearing customs, but with the signs in Japanese and most of the people being Japanese, it was a different experience. She would have liked to explore Japan and learn more about it, but she wasn't here as a tourist. On the immigration form she had checked "Business" as the purpose of her visit since that was the closest choice they gave her. She wondered if the official who examined her form would have blinked if she had written that the purpose of her visit was to take home her twelve-year-old daughter who had been kidnapped and sold as a sex slave.

Two hours after the plane landed they checked into their hotel, where they stayed only long enough to make sure their luggage was in their room and to get Bo, whom she had packed among her clothes. The bear no longer smelled like Amanda.

By then it was four, the day after they left New York, and neither of them had slept on the flight, so they were operating on adrenaline. With frayed nerves they left their room, went down to the lobby, and asked the concierge to get a taxi.

A half hour later they arrived at the office of the organization that Jeanne worked with, having no idea where they were in the city. All Carol remembered of the ride was a lot of signs in Japanese, a lot of traffic, and a lot of people.

They were greeted by a young woman who treated them very politely and acted as if she was expecting them. Before they boarded the plane in New York, knowing the flight would depart on time, Carol had called Jeanne to let her know their expected

164

time of arrival in Tokyo, and Jeanne had said she would make an appointment for them at five. So they were early.

"If you will please wait a moment," the receptionist said, "I will get the doctor."

The young woman made a phone call, speaking in Japanese.

They waited, standing in front of her desk, and within a few minutes a woman who looked in her mid-thirties came through a door. She was wearing an open white lab coat over her dress, and she approached them purposefully.

"I'm Doctor Kimura," she said, presenting a card to Carol with a slight bow.

"I'm glad to meet you," Carol said, looking at the card, which told her the doctor's full name was Hiroko Kimura, and that her specialty was pediatrics.

"I thought it would be a good idea if we talked before you see your daughter. We can go into my office."

"Okay," Carol said, having noticed that the doctor spoke perfect English with an accent like Jeanne's, though it also had a tinge of the south.

They followed the doctor into a small office that was sparely furnished with four cane chairs around a glass table. There was no desk, and there were no file cabinets. There was only a manila envelope on the table.

"You can call me Hiroko," the doctor said as they sat down.

"Where did you learn English?" Carol asked her.

"I studied medicine at the University of Cincinnati," Hiroko said. "They have a good program in pediatrics, which is what I wanted, and I lived there for almost ten years."

That explained the accent.

"Did you examine our daughter?" Brian asked.

"Yes. I did," Hiroko said "There's a copy of my report in that envelope, which you can give to her doctors at home. If it's okay with you, I'll tell you directly what I found."

"It's okay with us," Carol said.

"I found damage to her vagina, which I expected, but I also found damage to her anus."

"God damn them," Brian growled.

"After all the damage I've seen," Hiroko said with subdued fury, "I should be used to it. But I'm not. In fact, the more I see, the more I favor capital punishment for the men who do this kind of thing."

"How bad is the damage?" Carol asked.

"The physical damage won't be permanent."

"What about the mental damage?"

"That's another matter." Hiroko paused, and then she said: "I'm not a psychiatrist, so I can't give you an official diagnosis. But from what I've seen of girls who had a similar experience, your daughter has symptoms of post-traumatic stress disorder."

"You mean like the troops who come back from a war?"

"Since our country isn't in a war, I haven't seen any of them. But I've read about them, and I'd say your daughter's condition is similar."

"How bad is she?" Brian asked.

"You'll see in a moment. I just wanted to prepare you so you wouldn't be shocked."

"I'm ready for anything," Carol said, hoping she was.

"Well, I should warn you, she hasn't said a word since we rescued her. She might break her silence when she sees you, but she might not. So don't rush her."

"We won't," Brian said.

"I brought her bear," Carol said. "I've been sleeping with him since she went missing. He smelled like her, but now he smells like me. Do you think I should give him to her?"

"I think you should offer him to her," Hiroko said, "and see what she does."

"Okay. I'll try that."

"I'll go and get her now," Hiroko said, rising. "She's sharing a bedroom with another girl, so you'll have more privacy here."

As they waited for Hiroko to return with their daughter Carol laid her hand on Brian's shoulder. "Are you okay?"

"Yeah. Are you?" He put his hand on hers.

"I said I was ready for anything, but I don't know. I guess I won't know until I see her."

"With our love we can heal her," Brian reminded her.

"Yeah, I know." But she was beginning to wonder.

Hiroko returned, holding Amanda's hand and guiding her as if she was blind.

They both got up and went around the table.

The main thing Carol noticed about her daughter was the blank look in her green eyes, and for a moment she was afraid that Amanda didn't recognize them. But then there was a flicker, and Amanda rushed forward to take Bo and press him to her face. She smelled the bear, inhaling deeply, and when she looked up there were tears in her eyes.

"Oh, honey," Carol said, hugging her.

Brian joined them, wrapping his arms around them.

When they had disengaged themselves, Carol asked: "Can we take her with us now?"

"You can," Hiroko said. "You just have to sign a paper."

As they were about to leave the office Amanda jumped as if someone had jabbed her in the back, and her mouth flew open.

Carol then noticed that they had removed Amanda's braces.

In the taxi returning to the hotel Amanda held Bo tightly and buried her face in her mother's lap as if to prevent herself from seeing the city around her. Carol kept an arm around her and didn't take her eyes off her.

When they arrived at the hotel they guided Amanda into an elevator, but just before the doors closed a pair of Japanese businessmen barged into the car, and at the sight of them Amanda let out a shrill scream. Understanding her daughter's reaction, Carol shielded her from the men and glared at them, silently warning them to turn around and look only at the doors of the elevator. Luckily, they got out at the next floor.

In the room, which had two queen size beds, Amanda walked over to the television and found the remote and turned it on. It was tuned to a Japanese news program, and at the sound of men talking in Japanese she dropped the remote and rushed to her mother, still holding Bo.

While Carol comforted her, Brian retrieved the remote and muted the sound.

"See if you can get MTV," Carol suggested.

It took him a few minutes to get it, and the screen showed a teenage American girl singing. He unmuted the sound, and they heard the music that Amanda and her friends usually listened to. It was rife with sexual innuendo, but now it seemed so innocent.

Amanda sat down at the foot of the nearest bed and gazed intently at the television.

"We're going to order room service," Carol told her. "What would you like?"

Amanda said nothing, keeping her eyes on the screen.

"Would you like a cheeseburger?"

Amanda shrugged as if it didn't matter.

Carol picked up the phone and ordered two hamburgers and one cheeseburger, all well done, with French fries and a side order of mayonnaise, which Amanda preferred to catsup for her fries and Carol liked with tomato and lettuce on her burger.

"Since we're not going out," she told Amanda, "you can put on your pajamas."

Amanda didn't say anything, but she got up and headed toward the bathroom. Carol followed her bringing the pajamas and wishing she was only going into a try-on room to help her daughter make a decision.

Inside the bathroom Amanda exchanged the bear for the pajamas and stripped to her panties, handing each item to Carol, who noticed that she had lost weight to the point where her ribs stood out. In fact, she looked like a starving waif, and it was impossible for Carol to imagine how anyone could look at this emaciated body as a sex object.

After putting on the light blue top and the pink pants with kittens on them Amanda looked more like her old self.

"You feel better?" Carol asked.

Amanda nodded, but still didn't talk.

They returned to the bedroom, where Amanda reoccupied her place at the foot of the bed and gazed at the television with an arm locked on Bo.

They ate their burgers at the table where business travelers could work using the internet connection the hotel provided. Amanda ate heartily, which prompted Carol to ask: "How long since you had a cheeseburger?"

Amanda shrugged as if she didn't know, and that left Carol wondering what her captors had been feeding her.

When they had cleaned off the table Carol got out Amanda's computer, and for the next hour or so while she and Brian watched a news program Amanda sat at the table playing on her computer. It seemed to relax her, and evidently she didn't find anything on her Facebook that upset her.

During that time Carol sent text messages to Saša and Jeanne telling them that Amanda was in their hotel room with them, and asking Jeanne to make an appointment for Amanda to see a doctor the day after they returned. It was seven in the morning New York time so she didn't expect a reply until later.

Since they were completely exhausted, they went to bed by nine. Amanda slept with Carol, with Bo between them, and Brian took the other bed.

Around three in the morning Amanda woke them, screaming: "No, please! No, please!"

Carol held her terrified daughter, saying: "It's all right, honey. It's all right. They're not going to hurt you ever again."

"Don't let them," Amanda pleaded.

"I won't. I promise." Unable to see how satisfying her need to confess would benefit her daughter, she didn't say: "I'm so sorry I let it happen."

Their flight home was scheduled to depart at shortly after six the next evening, but they slept late and they had to be at the airport two hours early, so they didn't have too much time to kill. They arrived at the airport an extra hour early, and that turned out to be a good thing since the man at immigration noticed that Amanda's passport didn't show her entering Japan.

"There's a simple explanation for that," Brian told the man. "Would you like to hear it?"

"Yes. I would like to hear it," the man said.

Brian leaned toward him and whispered into his ear so Amanda couldn't hear it.

The man's eyes popped and his jaw dropped as if he had been punched in the stomach. But then he asked: "Do you have any evidence of that?"

"As a matter of fact I do," Brian said grimly. He opened the bag that was slung over his shoulder and started to take out the envelope from Doctor Kimura.

"All right. I believe you," the man said, not wanting to see the contents of the envelope. He stamped Amanda's passport and gestured them to move on.

The flight home was long and uneventful. Amanda was occupied watching the movies that Carol selected for her, one after another for a total of five. Though Carol watched them with her, if only to share an experience with her daughter, she couldn't have said afterward what the movies were about. But they seemed to entertain Amanda.

Though the flight had taken twelve hours, they magically arrived in New York at the same time they left Tokyo. By the time they went through immigration and cleared customs and got their baggage it was after seven. The driver they had scheduled to pick them up was waiting for them, and they were home by shortly after eight.

As soon as they were in the house Carol led Amanda upstairs to the familiar surroundings of her room, where she watched her move around, stopping at objects of furniture and touching them as if to make sure they were real.

"You're home," Carol assured her.

Amanda kept moving around and touching things.

In the meantime Brian had gone to get Matthew at his

friend's house, and Carol was still in her daughter's room when she heard her son running upstairs.

"Hey, Amanda," he said, coming into her room and acting as if she too had been at a friend's house. "Welcome home!"

She stared at him and stepped behind her mother's body for protection.

"It's your brother Matthew," Carol told her.

Still staring at her brother, she stood like a cat seeing another cat invade its territory.

"I'm sorry," Matthew said, backing off.

"No, it's all right," Carol said. "She's not used to seeing you. Maybe you should leave us for a while."

"Okay." He hesitated, and before leaving them he said: "I love you, Amanda."

Amanda took her hand as if she was seeking verification of this statement, and Carol gave her an affirmative hug, wanting also to hug her son for what he had said.

When they had completed an inventory of the room she asked Amanda: "Are you hungry?"

Amanda shrugged in a way that left open the possibility that she might be hungry.

"Let's go down to the kitchen," she said, leading the way.

Amanda tagged along docilely. She had never been unruly, but she had never been docile either, so her willingness to go along with whatever Carol suggested was a notable and somewhat disturbing change.

They found Brian and Matthew in the kitchen talking about baseball.

By now it was almost eight thirty, and since it was too late to cook anything Carol decided to order pizza. She assumed that Amanda hadn't had pizza since before they had gone on vacation, and that it would be like comfort food. But her children had different preferences: while Matthew liked his pizza with sausage, Amanda liked hers with pepperoni.

Just to make sure, she asked Amanda: "Would you like yours with pepperoni?"

Amanda nodded slowly. "Okay."

So she ordered two small pies, one of them half with sausage and half with pepperoni and the other with fresh garlic.

In the meantime her son had brought a Sudoku pad to the table and offered it to Amanda. They both liked the game, and after starting with a mini version they had graduated to a regular version at a low level of difficulty.

Conscious of the fact that the game was Japanese and might upset Amanda, Carol held her breath while Amanda stared at the pad as if she didn't recognize it.

"You played Sudoku all the time. Remember?" Matthew said. He wrote a number to help her get started.

Amanda took the pencil from him and wrote a number on the pad. It was clear from Matthew's expression that the number made absolutely no sense, but he didn't say anything. He let her write numbers randomly.

Brian and Matthew resumed talking about baseball, debating whether Hughes or Garcia should be kept in the rotation, and then they left to pick up the pizzas.

While they were gone Carol called her mother.

"Hello," her mother said with the accent on the first syllable, conveying the message that any phone call was an intrusion.

"We're home."

"Thank God. How's Amanda?"

"She's fine," Carol said, conscious of Amanda sitting at the table across from her.

"Is she with you now?" her mother asked, understanding why she wasn't speaking freely.

"Yes. We're in the kitchen waiting for the guys to come back with pizza."

"You eat a lot of pizza," her mother said critically.

"We just got home. There wasn't time to cook anything."

"Is Amanda going to see a doctor?"

"We have an appointment for tomorrow."

"Is she going back to school?"

"Eventually, but I need to hear what the doctor says."

"Well, if you want us to stay with her while you're at work, we're always available."

"Thanks, mom. I'll let you know as soon as we know what's happening."

Involved in the task of writing numbers on the pad, Amanda could have been anywhere. But at least now she was safe at home, where those men couldn't hurt her. And Carol kept repeating to herself what she had said to Brian: "With our love we can heal her."

After carefully picking every piece of pepperoni off her half of the pizza, Amanda ate it and seemed to enjoy it. No one asked her what was wrong with the pepperoni.

That night Amanda slept with Carol, and Brian slept in Amanda's room since there wasn't room for three of them in the queen size bed.

In the middle of the night Amanda started screaming: "No, please! No, please!"

"It's all right, honey," Carol told her, holding her tight. It took all the faith she had, and then some, to believe what she was saying.

"God damn them," Brian said, standing in the doorway.

"Did she have a nightmare?" Matthew asked, standing beside him unwaveringly.

"Yes," his father told him. "She had a nightmare."

"Don't let them hurt me," Amanda pleaded.

"I won't. I promise," Carol said, wondering if a parent could ever keep such a promise.

Their appointment with the doctor was at ten the next morning. Carol let Amanda sleep as late as possible, but then she had to get her up. Like most children that age Amanda had trouble getting up in the morning, but already Carol sensed a change. The problem before was that Amanda just didn't feel like getting up, but now she didn't *want* to get up. She wanted to avoid facing whatever the day might bring.

"Come on, honey. You have to get up," Carol coaxed her.

"We have an appointment with a nice woman."

Amanda rolled away, clinging to Bo.

"She only wants to talk with you, and afterward you can have ice cream."

"I don't want ice cream," Amanda said contrarily.

"Then you can have whatever you want."

"I don't want anything. Let me sleep."

"You can take a nap this afternoon, but you have to get up now. Your father bought cupcakes from the bakery in town, and you can have one for breakfast."

"I don't want a cupcake."

"He got lemon and chocolate, your favorite flavors."

Amanda pulled the pillow over her head as if to drown out any temptations.

Carol gently but firmly lifted Amanda from the bed, wincing at how fragile her daughter had become. It was like picking up a baby bird.

A half hour later they were in the car heading toward Yonkers. In one hand Amanda held her bear and in the other a lemon cupcake.

Carol found a parking place on Riverdale, and they walked to the center.

Jeanne came out and welcomed them. She led them to an office and introduced them to a woman in her early forties who had sad brown eyes.

"This is Dr. Aronson," Jeanne said.

"You can call me Toby," the woman said.

Jeanne left them, and Carol and Amanda sat on a sofa while Toby pulled up a chair.

"I see you brought a friend with you," Toby said to Amanda. "What's his name?"

"His name is Bo."

"Do you sleep with him?"

"Yeah. And with my mother."

"Amanda," Toby said casually, "would it be all right with you if I asked your mother to let me talk with you and Bo?"

"You mean without her?"

"Yes, only for a while. And she'll be just outside the door."

Amanda looked at Carol, and Carol nodded to let her know it was all right with her, and then Amanda said: "Okay."

Carol got up from the sofa and rested a hand on Amanda's shoulder and kissed the top of her head, saying: "I won't be far away. Don't worry."

When she closed the door behind her, she saw Sonia sitting in one of the three chairs in the waiting area, and she guessed Jeanne had sent her there.

"How are you doing?" Sonia asked.

"I don't know," Carol said, sitting down.

"We focus on the victims, but sometimes we forget about the parents. Of course in many cases the parents are responsible for what happened, but in your case—"

"I feel responsible. I let it happen."

"You didn't prevent it from happening, but you didn't make it happen."

"What do you mean?"

"You didn't abuse her," Sonia explained. "You didn't drive her away from home looking for someone to care about her, like the mothers of most of our girls did."

"You mean Amanda knows I care about her."

"Yeah. And she trusts you."

"So you think I can help her."

"I know you can."

She patted Sonia on the arm gratefully.

"Toby will talk with Amanda alone, and then she'll talk with you alone. I'm here to keep you and Amanda company while you're waiting."

"You're good company," Carol said. "How long have you been working here?"

"Since the summer before my senior year in college," Sonia said. "I came here as an intern. Sister Maura found the position for me."

175

"Oh, yeah. She told me she belongs to a group of old nuns who got involved in the issue of human trafficking."

"They're not old. They're so full of energy. And they do so much for us."

"Well, maybe I can do something for you."

"I'm sure you *can* do something for us. But you don't have to think about that now."

"I do have to. I have to believe I'll get through this."

"You will," Sonia assured her.

They were sitting in a comfortable silence when Toby opened the door and said: "Carol, I have your daughter's permission to talk with you alone."

Amanda came around her and stopped, seeing Sonia.

"This is Sonia," Carol said. "She's going to keep you company while I talk with Dr. Aronson."

"It won't take long," Toby said.

"I see you have a bear," Sonia said to Amanda.

"His name is Bo," Amanda said shyly.

"Well, come and sit down and tell me about him."

Carol went into the office and Toby closed the door behind them. They sat down, and Toby said: "She's a lovely child."

"I know," Carol said.

"Before I tell you what I think, I'd like you to tell me what you've observed about her behavior."

"You mean what's different about her behavior?"

"Whatever you've observed."

"Well, for one thing she's very anxious."

"I observed that too."

"There are times when she jumps for no apparent reason."

"How often does that happen?"

"Now and then," Carol said. "The first time it happened was in Tokyo while we were leaving the doctor's office. Her mouth flew open, and that's when I saw they'd removed her braces."

"It happened while she was talking with me," Toby said. "She jumped as if someone had jabbed her in the back."

"Yeah. That's what it's like."

"I think she has flashbacks."

"You mean flashbacks of what happened to her?"

"Yes. They don't last long because she represses them. She doesn't want to remember what happened to her."

"I can understand that," Carol said.

"What else have you observed?"

"She has nightmares, terrible nightmares."

"How often does she have them?" Toby asked.

"She's had them both nights that she's been with us."

"Can you tell me anything about them?"

"In her sleep she screams: 'No, please! No, please!' And I can imagine what that's about."

"I think we know what it's about. Does she wake up from the nightmares?"

"I wake her up," Carol said, "and I promise I won't let them hurt her ever again."

"Does she respond to that?"

"No, not really. But I have to believe it comforts her."

"I think it does," Toby said, "even if she doesn't know why you're trying to comfort her."

"You said she doesn't want to remember what happened to her? But *does* she remember what happened to her?"

"She says she doesn't. She says the last thing she remembers before you brought her home from Japan was having dinner at her grandparents' house."

"That was the Sunday before we went to St. Anselm," Carol said, trying to piece it together. "So she doesn't remember going to St. Anselm?"

"She says she doesn't, and I believe her. When people have a traumatic experience," Toby explained, "they often can't recall the events leading up to it."

"I assume that helping her recall those events isn't the first thing we want to do."

"It's the last thing we want to do. The first thing we want to do is to make her feel loved and secure."

"We're trying to make her feel loved and secure," Carol said.

"So let's review her symptoms," Toby said after a pause. "She's very anxious, she has flashbacks, and she has nightmares. Based on those symptoms and her general behavior, I think she has post-traumatic stress disorder."

"That's what the doctor in Tokyo thought."

"I see it often with these girls, especially the young ones who had no idea what they were getting into. In that sense they're like the boys who come back from our wars."

"What's the prognosis?" Carol asked, bracing herself.

"She has a long road ahead of her. She has to deal with feelings of anxiety, depression, and shame. And I'm sure she never had to deal with these feelings in a major way."

"She never did in a major way."

"Most of the victims I see are from different backgrounds," Toby said. "If they only have a mother, they were abused by her. If they have two parents, they were abused by both of them. They have zero or negative self-esteem, so they let pimps enslave them, abuse them, and take advantage of them. They feel they deserve to be treated like shit."

"If that's how they feel, then wouldn't it be harder for them to recover?"

"You'd think it would be, and honestly I haven't seen enough cases like your daughter's to make a valid comparison. But those victims have one advantage."

"What's that?"

"They're tough."

"I know what you mean," Carol said. "I grew up in a tough neighborhood. I had to deal with a lot things my daughter hasn't had to deal with."

"Where did you grow up?"

"In a bad area of Yonkers. I didn't know how bad it was, but it was bad, and it was getting worse."

Toby nodded. "So you wanted to raise your children in a better neighborhood."

"Yeah. I didn't want them to have to deal with street gangs.

But maybe I protected them too much. Maybe I should have exposed them more to the real world."

"What are you saying?"

"I'm saying I blame myself for protecting her. But at the same time I blame myself for taking my eyes off her on St. Anselm."

"You have a conflict," Toby said. "You blame yourself for protecting your children too much, and you blame yourself for not protecting them enough."

"So I have a conflict. Do I have to resolve it?"

"No. You only have to be aware of it."

"I'm aware of it," Carol said.

They were silent for a while, and then Toby said: "I can treat your daughter for anxiety. There's a drug that could help her."

"I don't like drugs."

"I don't recommend them lightly. But it could help her. It doesn't have major side effects, and it's not addictive."

"What else do you recommend?"

"I recommend therapy," Toby said. "There's a woman at the center who works with these girls. Her name is Heather."

"What about school?"

"I don't recommend it for a while. The kids all know what happened to her, and you can't expect them to understand and be sensitive about it. Just one remark could throw Amanda into a downward spiral."

"Could we have her do the schoolwork at home?"

"You could try," Toby said. "But she's going to have trouble concentrating. And she's probably not going to remember what she learned in the weeks before you went to St. Anselm."

"In other words, she should take the seventh grade over?"

"That might not be a bad thing. In many respects she has to start over, and if she took the seventh grade over at least she'd be with different kids."

"What about her friends?"

"Does she have many friends?"

"She has several, including a best friend."

"You know, I asked her if she had a best friend," Toby said, "and she shook her head adamantly."

"Her best friend was the girl who was kidnapped with her."

"Well, I don't think Amanda should see her for a while. That could bring back the traumatic experience, and I don't think she's ready to deal with it."

"Okay," Carol said, trying to assimilate everything. "Will you give me a prescription for the drug you mentioned?"

"I'll give it to you now. And I'll make an appointment for next week. Will the same time work for you?"

"Yes. It will. I really appreciate—"

"Don't say it. Wait until we make some progress."

With the prescription Carol left the office and found Amanda talking with Sonia. It didn't matter that they were talking about the bear's family in the high mountains where he had come from. The fact that Amanda was talking with someone gave Carol a shot of badly needed encouragement for the long road ahead.

On the way home she left the prescription at the pharmacy and then she went to the A&P, where along with the other things she needed she got an onion, ground beef, a container of ricotta, a can of imported whole tomatoes, and a box of ziti. She realized that her decision to make baked ziti for her family that evening was at least in part a reaction to her mother's comment about the pizza, but she also wanted something to do while she tried to process what the doctor had said about Amanda's condition.

As they moved up and down the aisles Amanda stuck by her, not running off as she usually did to find something that Carol wouldn't have thought of buying. Instead, she walked along holding the edge of the cart in one hand and Bo in the other.

Stopping in front of the ice cream, Carol asked her: "What flavor would you like?"

Amanda shrugged as if it didn't matter.

"Chocolate Fudge Brownie?"

"Okay," Amanda said.

When they had everything Carol headed for a checkout counter, avoiding the line where a neighbor was standing. She had nothing against the neighbor, but she didn't want to have a public conversation about Amanda.

Unfortunately, the woman spotted them and waited for them on the way out.

"I'm so happy you found her," the woman said.

"We got home last night," Carol said.

"Is she all right?" The woman glanced at Amanda as if she might be carrying a virus from the barnyards of Asia.

"Oh, yeah. She's fine," Carol said, putting a protective arm around her daughter.

As they followed the woman out into the parking lot Carol hoped they wouldn't run into anyone else she knew. She couldn't tell if Amanda had noticed the way the woman had glanced at her, and not knowing what to expect from people, her instinct was to protect Amanda from them.

By the time she returned to the pharmacy the prescription was ready, and she charged the co-pay to her medical card. It was forty dollars, indicating that the drug was expensive. If all the veterans with post-traumatic stress disorder were taking this drug, then the company that sold it was making a lot of money from the wars.

When they got home they went directly into the kitchen, where she put away the groceries and scooped some ice cream into a bowl for Amanda.

For a while she stood and watched her daughter eat the ice cream, taking a small amount at a time and licking it daintily off the spoon. And then she sat down at the table across from her and called the college.

Griselda answered and assured her that everything was in place for the Trustees' Dinner before passing the call to Tom.

"How are you doing?" Tom asked her.

"I don't know," she said. "We saw a doctor this morning, and we have an appointment with a therapist tomorrow."

"I think you should take a leave of absence."

"Well, I don't know how much time I'll need."

"You can take a few months and see how it goes."

"I could probably work from home."

"I think you should stop working," Tom advised her, "until you know more about your daughter's condition."

"Would I still get my health benefits?"

"Of course. And you'd still get your salary."

"How can you manage that?"

"I have you in my budget, and I don't plan to replace you."

"But what if I can't come back to work?"

"We'll deal with that if it happens. So don't think about it. Think about Amanda."

"Thanks, Tom."

"Is she with you now?"

"Oh, yeah. She's sitting across the kitchen table from me, eating Chocolate Fudge Brownie ice cream." The words caught the attention of Amanda, who looked up from the bowl and smiled at her sweetly.

"Chocolate Fudge Brownie? That sounds yummy."

"I'll bring some to you."

"Wait until my birthday."

She knew when his birthday was since they always gave a little party for him in the office. "Okay. I will. And thanks again."

After finishing the ice cream Amanda asked: "Can I go up to my room now?"

"Sure. Are you going to play on your computer?"

Amanda nodded.

Carol hesitated, wondering if she should accompany Amanda and help her get started, but she decided to give Amanda a little space, so she stayed in the kitchen. She had always tried to limit the time her children played on their computers since she didn't want them to spend their lives in the virtual world, but after her daughter's encounter with the real world she felt there were worse things children could be doing than playing on their computers.

She made coffee and sat down at the table, thinking about her conversation with Toby. She hadn't asked about the extent to which Amanda would recover since she knew it was a question that even with all her knowledge and experience, Toby couldn't answer. It depended on so many unknown variables. It was like raising children—you couldn't predict how they would come out, you could only love them no matter what happened.

TWELVE

SHE REACHED ACROSS the table and started going through the mail that had piled up since Friday. She was looking at the bill for car insurance, surprised that it was lower than the month before, when the phone rang.

It was Lindsey, who said: "I heard you found Amanda."

"Yeah." She didn't know how to handle this development. "How did you hear about it?"

"From my network. I'm *so* happy for you."

"I guess you want to know if you can announce it."

"That's right. I'm calling to get your permission—and to get an interview."

"You don't need my permission."

"I'd prefer to have it."

She thought for a moment. She didn't want the attention that would come from public knowledge of her daughter's rescue, but she also recognized that sooner or later everyone would know about it. And Lindsey had not only been helpful, she was also sensitive enough to want her permission to announce the news. So she said: "Okay. You have my permission. And I'll give you an interview, but not until I know more about my daughter's condition."

"I understand. My heart is with you."

"Thanks, Lindsey."

When she finished with the mail she still had most of the day ahead of her, with nothing to do, so she decided to start making the baked ziti. She filled a big pot with water, shook some salt into it, and turned the flame to high. She put the box of ziti next to the stove, ready to empty the contents into the boiling water. She then opened the can of tomatoes. Though they were more expensive than domestic tomatoes, her mother had always stretched the budget to use them, insisting that there was nothing like the taste of a tomato grown in Italy.

While she was waiting for the water to boil she chopped the onion and scraped it off the cutting board into a skillet. She added the light olive oil she used for cooking and turned on the burner under the skillet. She cooked the onion until it was translucent, and then she added three cloves of finely chopped garlic, which she cooked for only about a minute. Next she added the ground beef, which she broke up with a fork and cooked until it was completely browned. After chopping the tomatoes she added them along with salt, pepper, oregano, and a teaspoon of sugar. She stirred the sauce and covered the skillet and turned the heat down to low.

With the water boiling vigorously she dumped the ziti into the pot and quickly stirred it with the claw-like utensil to prevent the tubes of pasta from sticking together. For that purpose she didn't put oil into the water as some people did since her mother frowned on it, saying it was no substitute for watching the pasta and stirring it.

From time to time over the next twenty minutes she tested the pasta, lifting a tube out of the water with a fork and blowing on it and biting it. When it was ready she poured the pot into a colander in the sink, shook the pasta to get rid of all the water, and then emptied it into a bowl, where she tossed it with oil.

She checked the sauce, tasting it and grinding a little more pepper into it, and then she went upstairs to see how Amanda was doing. At the top of the stairs she heard the shower, and she rushed to the bathroom door and opened it.

Through the steamy air she saw Amanda's clothes scattered on the floor.

"Are you in the shower?" she asked fearfully.

"Yeah," Amanda said.

"Are you all right?"

"Yeah."

It was the first time in her life that Amanda had voluntarily taken a shower.

Finding a reason to stay in the bathroom, Carol knelt down and picked up the clothes. She looked for signs of blood in the panties and was relieved to find none. "Can I get you some fresh clothes?"

"Okay." There was a pause as if Amanda was going to say what she wanted to wear, but the silence went on indefinitely.

Carol put the dirty clothes into the hamper and left the bathroom and went to Amanda's room and got a clean pair of jeans, a top, and panties. When she returned to the bathroom Amanda was still in the shower.

She hung the clothes on a hook and debated whether to stay in the bathroom until Amanda came out of the shower. Deciding not to stay, she told Amanda: "I'm going to lie down for a while. You're welcome to join me."

Amanda didn't acknowledge her invitation, but a few minutes after Carol lay down on the bed they now shared Amanda joined her, snuggling next to her with Bo between them. Amanda hadn't dried her hair, which smelled of shampoo.

"I love you, honey," Carol said, holding her tenderly.

"I love you too," Amanda said.

Though Amanda said this sadly, Carol still considered it a major breakthrough—at least those brutes hadn't erased from her daughter's heart the notion of love.

When they returned to the kitchen after their nap the sauce was ready, so she mixed it with the pasta and poured it into a baking dish. She mixed the ricotta into it, sprinkled it with ground Parmesan, dotted it with butter, and covered it.

By then Matthew was home from school, and instead of rushing up to his bedroom to play on his computer, he lingered in the kitchen.

Amanda was sitting at the table with the Sudoku pad he had given her the night before.

"How are you doing?" Matthew asked her.

Amanda shrugged as if she didn't know.

He leaned over and checked the numbers she was putting into the squares. He seemed about to make a suggestion, but then he looked at Carol for guidance.

She nodded, indicating she thought it would be all right for him to help his sister.

"Why don't you try the seven?" he suggested to her.

She stopped, tightening her grip on Bo.

"I don't know if it'll work," he said, "but why don't you try it and see? Okay?"

She wrote down a seven. From the expression on her face it was impossible to tell if she knew what she was doing.

They were still working together on the puzzle when Brian got home, early.

"Hey, guys," he said. "How's it going?"

"Fine," Matthew said, speaking for both of them.

"We're having baked ziti," Carol told him.

"That sounds good," he said. "I hope we're all hungry."

He came over and gave her a hug, and then he got a beer out of the refrigerator and sat down at the table with the kids.

Since he was home, she turned on the oven. She couldn't bring him up to date in front of the kids, but she could do that later. Now it was important for them to be together as a family so they could try to pick up where they had left off.

"Guess what," Brian said. "I got tickets to a Yankees game."

"You did?" Matthew said, excited. "When is it?"

"It's May 19th, in the afternoon. I figure that by then it should be warm enough to sit in the stadium."

"Who are we playing?"

"We're playing the Reds."

"They're supposed to be good."

"Can Bo go with us?" Amanda asked.

"Sure," Brian said, looking as if he had just received an unexpected blessing. "As long as he wears his Jeter shirt."

"He has to wear it. He doesn't have anything else to wear."

"So the five of us will go to a game."

"Bo doesn't need a ticket, does her?" Matthew asked, playing along with them.

"How old is he?" Brian asked Amanda.

"He's nine," Amanda said.

That was correct, Carol thought. Amanda had been three when they gave her the bear, and that was nine years ago.

"Then he can get in free," Brian said.

While the ziti was quietly baking in the oven they talked about baseball, speculating on how long it would take Pettitte to get back into action and join the rotation.

Amanda didn't participate in the conversation, but she seemed to listen.

After dinner, with the kids upstairs playing on their computers, she told Brian about her meeting with Toby. He listened without interrupting her until she got to the drug for anxiety, and then he asked: "What are the side effects?"

"Here," she said, reaching for the prescription, which she had left on top of the refrigerator. "You can read them."

"Let's see," he said, examining the information that came with the drug. "The *common* side effects are blurred vision, changes in sexual function, constipation, dizziness, drowsiness, dry mouth, gas, headache, increased appetite, lightheadedness, stomach pain, trouble concentrating, and weight gain."

"It seems like all drugs have those same side effects."

"Do we want to know the *severe* side effects?"

"Yeah, let's hear them."

"Severe allergic reactions, such as rashes, hives, itching, difficulty breathing, tightness in the chest, swelling of the mouth, face, lips, or tongue, unusual hoarseness—"

"Okay. I get the idea. But keep that so we can consult it if anything happens."

"I assume the benefits outweigh the side effects, but I don't know. Do you trust this doctor?"

"I trust her. She's serving the center as a volunteer."

"You mean apart from her regular practice."

"She has to make a living somehow."

Brian was silent for a while, and then he asked: "When would Amanda start taking this drug?"

"I thought tonight before she goes to bed. She'll be with me."

"Well, I guess that's all right," Brian said. "They didn't say it causes sleeplessness."

"If it reduces her anxiety, she might not have nightmares."

"That would be good. I mean, I think it would be. Don't nightmares have some psychological function?"

"I think they help us process things," Carol said, "but I don't remember what they do. When we see the therapist tomorrow I'll ask her about that."

Amanda took the drug before going to bed that night, and lying next to Carol she went to sleep almost right away. But in the middle of the night she started screaming: "No, please! No, please!" And Carol held her, promising not to let them hurt her ever again.

The next morning Carol was sitting at the kitchen table having a second cup of coffee after Matthew had left for school and Brian for work when the doorbell rang. It was a manual bell of the type used before there was electricity, and sometimes people stood at the door looking for a button to press and not seeing the brass key on the door that you turned to make the bell ring. Since Carol wasn't expecting anyone, she couldn't imagine who it was—she hoped it wasn't a proselytizer with the mission of saving her soul.

If only to stop the bell from ringing and waking Amanda, whom she had left upstairs asleep since their appointment with the therapist wasn't until one thirty that afternoon, she got up from the table and hurried to the front door. Through the glass that was shrouded with antique lace she could make out the head of a woman.

When she opened the door she saw it was Donna, who looked distraught.

"I wanted to catch you before you went to work," Donna said meekly.

"I'm not working," Carol said. "I took a leave of absence."

"Well, I heard on the news that you found Amanda."

They hadn't watched Lindsey's announcement because she was afraid it would upset Amanda. "Yeah, we found her."

"How is she?" Donna asked with a look of fear.

"She's not a happy girl," Carol said after trying to find an apt way to put it.

"I'm so sorry." Tears were already beginning to form in Donna's wide eyes.

"Would you like to come in?"

Donna hesitated as if she was afraid of what she might encounter. "Oh, I don't know if I should. I mean—"

"Come on," Carol encouraged her, stepping back from the doorway to let her pass.

Donna came into the house and followed her though the hall to the kitchen.

"Would you like some coffee?"

"No, thanks. I gave it up."

"I should give it up."

They sat down at the table, where they had sat so many times in the past. It was hard now for Carol to believe that they had been friends.

"Where's Amanda?" Donna asked.

"She's upstairs sleeping."

"That's good." Donna paused. "Stacy has trouble sleeping. She feels bad about what happened."

"Why does Stacy feel bad? It wasn't her fault."

"She feels it was. It was her idea to leave the resort."

"I thought she said it was Amanda's idea."

"She did say that, but she was lying."

This information had different effects on Carol's feelings. It made her feel better about her daughter's role in what had happened, but it made her feel worse about the Walkers' refusal to let their daughter talk with Frank. "When did Stacy tell you it was her idea?"

"While we were discussing whether or not we should let her talk with Frank."

"And what was her position?"

"She wanted to talk with him," Donna said. "And she finally told us why she felt she should. She believed that what happened was her fault."

"But you wouldn't let her talk with him."

"We were afraid that if we let her talk with him *they would kill our children*," Donna said with her voice rising.

"I understand." She didn't point out that if Stacy had talked with Frank they might have found Amanda in time.

"So now," Donna said, "she has to live with the feeling that she should have talked with Frank."

"But she wanted to talk with him," Carol pointed out, "and she would have if you'd let her."

"I know, and I keep telling her that, but it doesn't help."

"Well, I don't know what to tell you."

After a long pause Donna said: "I thought it might help if she talked with Amanda."

"It might," Carol said, resisting the idea. "But Amanda's doctor doesn't think she should see Stacy for a while."

"What kind of doctor?"

"A psychiatrist. She has a lot of experience in treating victims of sex slavery."

"I hope Amanda wasn't—" Donna broke off, unable to bring herself to say the word.

"She was. She was raped."

"Oh, God," Donna said, clapping her hand to her mouth. "I'm so sorry."

"The doctor's afraid that if she sees Stacy it'll bring back the traumatic experience," Carol explained, "and she doesn't think Amanda's ready to deal with it."

Donna sighed. "Then I guess we'll have to wait."

Carol could see that like Donna a week ago she was in a position where she didn't want to risk her own daughter's safety in order to help her friend's daughter. But she did come up with an idea. "It might help Stacy if she talked with Frank and gave him evidence that Ramsey could use to put away those Russians so they won't hurt any more girls."

"I can see how that might relieve her conscience," Donna said, nodding.

"Suggest it to her," Carol said, feeling she had found the right solution. "And when Amanda's ready, they can talk about what happened."

When Donna had gone Carol went up to check on Amanda. At the top of the stairs she heard the shower running, and though it didn't alarm her as it had yesterday, it still concerned her. The girl who had resisted taking showers now evidently had a compulsion to take them, and Carol could imagine why. She opened the bathroom door and asked: "Are you okay?"

"Yeah, I'm okay," Amanda said.

Deciding not to interfere, Carol went into her bedroom and made the bed and sat the bear on Amanda's pillow with his back resting against the headboard.

She went to Amanda's room and puttered around until she finally heard the shower stop. She hadn't timed it, but she figured that Amanda had been in the shower at least a half hour.

The door of the bathroom opened, and Amanda emerged in a cloud of steam, already dressed. Her hair was dripping wet.

"You should use the drier," Carol told her.

"I don't need it," Amanda said, heading for the room where she slept.

From the hall Carol watched her go to the bed and pick up Bo and give him a hug. With the bear in hand she came out of the room and headed for the room where she used to sleep but where she now kept her clothes and played on her computer.

"You don't have time to play on the computer. We have an appointment at one thirty, and you have to eat something."

"I'm not hungry."

"You will be hungry. Come on, let's go." She put an arm around Amanda's shoulder and gently guided her toward the stairs without any further resistance.

In the kitchen Amanda asked: "Can I have French toast?"

"Sure," Carol said. She had bought a loaf of filone at the supermarket, and while Amanda sat at the table gazing at the Sudoku pad she cut three slices of the bread and soaked them in a mixture of eggs, cream, salt, pepper, and vanilla. She got out the griddle she used for pancakes and put it on a burner and turned the flame to high.

"I feel clean now," Amanda said.

"You *are* clean. You just took a shower."

"I had to take one because I felt dirty."

"That's okay. You can take a shower whenever you feel like it."

Amanda nodded and wrote on the Sudoku pad.

At one they left the house and headed for Yonkers. They were waiting at Five Corners for the light to change when Amanda said: "I can't find my phone. Have you seen it?"

"No," Carol said, not wanting to go anywhere near where this question would lead.

"I can't remember what I did with it."

"You might have lost it. But don't worry. If you did lose it, we'll buy you another phone. What kind do you want?"

"The kind I had. I wish I could remember what I did with it."

Carol let the subject drop, and within a few minutes Amanda turned on the radio and found the station the kids listened to. For the past few years Amanda had sung along with the music, using words she didn't understand, but now as they played a song she must have heard a hundred times she only listened.

At the center Sonia greeted them and led them to an office and introduced them to Heather, a young black woman with compassionate eyes and rows of tightly braided hair running from the front to the back of her head.

"I'm glad to meet you," she told Amanda, not shaking her

hand but taking it and holding it. "Will you introduce me to your friend here?"

"His name is Bo," Amanda said without reservation.

"That's a perfect name for him."

"Did you ever have a bear?"

"Yeah, I still have him."

"What's his name?"

"His name is Marley."

"Where is he?"

"Oh, he's at home sitting on my bed."

"Why is he there?"

"To watch my bed and make sure no one steals it. And you know what? Since he's been watching it, no one has stolen it."

"Then he must be good at watching your bed."

"He is. And I'm sure Bo is good at doing what he does."

"He hangs out with me," Amanda said, holding him against the side of her face.

"Could I talk with her alone for a while?" Heather asked.

"Is that okay with you?" Carol asked Amanda.

Amanda nodded. "It's okay with me."

After kissing Amanda softly on her forehead, Carol left her and went with Sonia to the waiting area, where they sat down.

"I heard an accent," Carol said. "Where's Heather from?"

"Jamaica," Sonia told her. "But she's been around. When she was thirteen her mother sold her to get money for drugs."

"Her mother *sold* her?"

"That's what happens when drugs become more important than children. There are women who have children just for the purpose of selling them to get money for drugs."

"I can't imagine women doing that."

"I couldn't either, but they do."

"So Heather was a sex slave?"

"For six years. She spent most of that time in Germany."

"How did she escape?"

"One of our sister organizations rescued her. They brought her to New York, and with their help she pursued her education.

She just completed a doctor's degree in psychology."

"Does she have a family?"

"These girls are her family. She lives for them."

After about forty-five minutes the door opened, and Heather gently guided Amanda out while inviting Carol to come in. Reassured by Amanda's peaceful look, Carol left her with Sonia and went into the office.

"I won't keep you in suspense," Heather said as soon as they had sat down. "I believe we can help Amanda, but it's going to take a while."

"Do you mean months? Years?"

"It's going to take years, but at least she has something to build on."

"What does she have?"

"The love you gave her from the day she was born. Most of the girls we rescue didn't get that love, so they have little or nothing to build on."

Carol had a feeling that Heather was speaking not only from her experience as a therapist but also from her experience as a child whose mother sold her for drugs. "So Amanda has something to build on. What would we build?"

"A new Amanda," Heather said.

"Then it wouldn't be the old Amanda?"

"After what happened to her she'll never be the same."

"But something will be left of the old Amanda."

"Oh, yes," Heather assured her. "We want her to get in touch with the old Amanda. But there's a gap between where she is now and where she was before."

"Has her memory been erased?"

"I don't think it's been erased. I think it's inaccessible."

"Are you going to help her access it?"

"Not yet. I'm going to help her move ahead, and if all goes well someday she'll be able to deal with what happened. But I'm going to proceed carefully," Heather added. "She's close to the edge of a deep hole."

From hearing Amanda cry out in those nightmares Carol

understood the therapist's concern. It was her concern when she held her daughter and promised not to let them hurt her ever again. "So what can I do to keep her from falling?"

"You can love her unconditionally."

"Isn't that what parents are supposed to do?"

"It is. But not all parents love their children that way."

"I love my daughter unconditionally," Carol said, affirming a belief that until the past few weeks had never really been tested.

"Then you can help her," Heather said.

"Do you agree with Dr. Aronson that she shouldn't go back to school for a while?"

"Yes, I do," Heather said. "She'd be lost academically, and she'd have problems socially."

"But she has to do something. I don't want her to spend the whole day playing on her computer."

"Playing on her computer is all right up to a point. It enables her to avoid thinking about what happened. But it won't help her move ahead."

"What will help her?"

"Being with you, and doing things she did before."

"Well, I took a leave of absence from my job," Carol said, "so I can be with her all day. I just don't have a clear idea of what I should do with her."

"You should talk with her and hang out with her and work with her on things she'd be doing at school, like reading, writing, and arithmetic."

"Do you have a program I could follow?"

"I can give you books at her level," Heather said, "but you don't have to follow a program. You just have to help her apply her mind."

"What about physical exercise? She likes tennis."

"If she plays tennis with you, okay. But I don't think she should play with friends yet."

Carol reconsidered. "She was playing tennis with her best friend before they went missing, so maybe it's not a good idea."

"Did she play tennis regularly?"

"She played all year round. We have a bubble in our village."

"Then if she plays with you, I don't think it would trigger anything." Heather paused, and then she asked: "What happened to the other girl?"

"Stacy? She escaped from the kidnappers before they could do any physical damage."

"Still, she had a terrifying experience, and she might also have survivor's guilt."

"She might," Carol said, knowing it had been Stacy's idea to leave the resort. "Her mother came to our house this morning and asked if Stacy could talk with Amanda. I told her the doctor didn't recommend that for a while."

"I don't recommend it either."

"But playing tennis with me is okay?"

"It should be okay. And it could help her get in touch with the old Amanda."

They made an appointment for the same time on Thursday, and they scheduled appointments on Tuesdays and Thursdays through the end of April.

Carol left the center with an armful of books that Heather had given her, and she drove home with Amanda, who listened to the music on the radio without singing. It was as if she had forgotten the words and was trying to relearn them.

When they got home the mailman was on the porch, about to put a bundle of letters into their box. He stopped and waited for them to approach.

At first Carol didn't recognize him, and then she realized it was Jimmy, who lived down the street in a house across from the garden apartments. His father, a plumber, worked for Brian on remodeling jobs, and his mother worked in the office of a family doctor in the village. Unlike the people who moved to Hastings for its schools, his parents had been born and raised here, and his father was a member of the volunteer fire department.

"Hi, Jimmy," she said, surprised to see him as a mailman. She had heard from Brian that he was back from Afghanistan after

197

serving a tour of duty there, and that he was having problems. But she hadn't seen him since before he was deployed. At the time she had felt he was the last young person they should send to war, a boy she had completely trusted as a baby-sitter when he was sixteen and her children were four and six.

"Hi, Mrs. Delaney," he said with the same kind of blank look that Amanda had.

"Are you our new mailman?"

"Yeah. They promoted Vincent."

"Well, they found a perfect replacement for him. You know the neighborhood."

"I do. But there are people I don't know."

She could understand why. The people who came here for the schools and didn't like paying taxes for other people's children sold their houses as soon as their own children graduated, and other people came here for the schools.

"You remember Jimmy, don't you?" she said to Amanda, who was half-hidden behind her. She brought Amanda forward with an arm around her shoulder.

"Hey, you still have Bo," Jimmy said with a look of pure joy.

"Hi, Jimmy," Amanda said, no longer acting shy of him.

"How are you guys doing?"

"We're doing okay."

He handed the bundle of letters to Carol, and then he said: "I have to go. I still have a lot of mail to deliver."

He was an hour later than Vincent. But after his exchange with Amanda she didn't care how late he delivered the mail.

Before dinner, while the kids were up in their rooms playing on their computers, she had some time alone with Brian in the kitchen, and she brought him up to date, telling him about the visit from Donna and the meeting with Heather.

"It sounds like Heather knows what she's doing," Brian said. "I just hope we don't lose much of the old Amanda."

"I hope we don't. But parents must always feel that way as their children grow up."

"This isn't about growing up. It's about dealing with evil. And Amanda shouldn't have to deal with evil at her age."

"It's not what we wanted for her," Carol agreed, "but a lot of kids have to deal with it. Heather was sold by her mother for drugs at the age of thirteen."

"She was?" Brian sighed. "Well, I don't want to sound like I think our daughter's better than those kids. I should have said *kids* shouldn't have to deal with evil at her age."

"I'm with you there."

They were silent for a while, and then he asked: "So are you going to play tennis with her?"

"I'm going to take her to the club tomorrow morning."

"Do you want me to join you?"

"No, you don't have to," Carol said. "But there *is* something you can do. She misses her phone, and she's trying to remember what she did with it."

"I assume we don't want her to remember."

"We don't until she's ready to deal with it. To stop her from worrying about her phone, I told her we'd buy her a new one. And she wants the kind she had before."

"I'll take her to the phone store tomorrow afternoon. But I don't know if we can get the same model she had before. They're always introducing new models."

"I think it's important to get the same model."

"I understand. Well, if the store doesn't have it," Brian said, "I can probably get it on eBay. If it's the same model, she won't care if it was reconditioned, will she?"

"As long as it's the same model I don't think she will. I couldn't tell that our landline phones were reconditioned."

That night Amanda cried out in her sleep, and Carol held her and promised not to let them hurt her ever again. She didn't know if this helped Amanda, or if Amanda even understood it, but she still did it, hoping that as a result of her reassurances Amanda would eventually stop having those nightmares.

The next morning, with difficulty, she got Amanda out of bed and on her feet by quarter after ten. In the hour and a half since Matthew and Brian left the house Carol had made lemon poppy seed muffins, which they all liked, and she gave one to Amanda for breakfast. Like the muffins she got at the bakery it had slivered almonds and sugar crumbs on top.

"Where are we going?" Amanda asked, eating the muffin.

"We're going to play tennis. Okay?"

"Okay. Where's my racket?"

"It's in your closet."

"I didn't see it there."

"It's probably behind some clothes, but it's there."

A few minutes later they went upstairs and found the racket. They changed into shorts and tee-shirts and sneakers, and then they left the house, Amanda with her racket in one hand and her bear in the other.

They drove down Southside Avenue and crossed the bridge that went over the railroad tracks and headed north on River Street, passing the last remaining building from the Anaconda complex. It was a typical red-brick plant from the era, with a saw-toothed roof. Its fate hadn't been decided, though there were people who wanted to preserve it and turn it into a museum. In the meantime it would take years and millions of dollars to clean up the pollution and get the site approved for development.

They parked across from the tennis club and entered the bubble-covered area. They had a court reserved for eleven, and they were five minutes early, so they had to wait for a couple of senior guys to finish. They looked as old as Carol's father, who she couldn't imagine playing tennis, and they relied on spin and placement instead of power to win points. As she watched them from the sidelines she realized that she could learn from their style of play.

"Okay, it's yours," the one with the head of hair said, leaving the court. He wasn't even breathing hard from their last rally.

"Thanks," she said. "You guys play well."

"You should have seen us when we were younger."

"We ran around a lot more then," the other guy said, rubbing his shoulder.

Amanda left Bo in a folding chair, in a position where if he had been a referee he could have called a let service.

Carol walked to the far court and bounced a ball until Amanda looked ready. Then with a long underhand stroke she put the ball into play.

It went to Amanda's backhand, but she returned it beautifully. She was one of the few girls her age with a classic one-handed backhand.

Carol had to move to get it, but she returned it, and the rally continued until she hit the ball into the net.

When they were warmed up they began a set, with Amanda serving. From the baseline Carol watched her serve, delighting in the way Amanda bent her knees before stretching up to hit the ball. It made her so happy that she forgot to follow the ball, which whizzed right by her.

"Hey, mom," the old Amanda yelled. "Were you ready?"

"Yeah, honey. You aced me."

The trip to the phone store that afternoon with Brian didn't go so well. They didn't have the same model that Amanda had before, and she became very upset about it. Brian had never seen her so upset, and he had to take her out of the store and sit her in the car and calm her down, assuring her that he would find the phone she wanted.

When they got home she went upstairs and took a long shower, which gave Brian the opportunity to tell Carol what had happened. It also gave him an opportunity to go on eBay and find the phone. By the time she joined them in the kitchen, with dripping wet hair, he could tell her: "I found it."

"Found what?" Amanda asked blankly.

"The phone you wanted."

"Oh. Where is it?"

"They're shipping it. You should have it by early next week."

"Okay. But what if I find the phone I lost?"

"You'll have two phones," Carol said as if there was a chance she might find it.

"If I do find it, then I'll give it to Bo."

"Do his friends have phones?"

"They all have phones. So he should have one."

"Well, if you don't find your old phone, you could share your new phone with him."

"I could," Amanda said as if she thought it was a good idea.

That night Amanda didn't cry out in her sleep. She slept so peacefully that Carol wondered if the exercise from playing tennis had done some good despite the setback at the phone store. And she resolved to keep playing tennis with Amanda.

The next morning, while Amanda was still sleeping and Carol was having a second cup of coffee at the kitchen table, the phone suddenly rang.

It was Frank, who said: "I have some news."

From his tone she could tell it was good news, but she couldn't imagine what it was.

"Stacy came and talked with me. She gave me information that'll help Ramsey make a case, and her mother's willing to let her testify at the trial of the Russians."

Though this development wouldn't help Amanda, it would help Stacy, and it would help the girls who might have been future victims of the Russians, so it made Carol feel good. She asked: "When's the trial?"

"It's late in May. She'll go with her mother to St. Anselm."

"I'm glad to hear that. I appreciate your telling me."

"How's your daughter doing?" Frank asked.

"She's doing all right, but the doctor says she has a long road ahead of her. She has post-traumatic stress disorder."

"I'm not surprised. I can't imagine what it was like for her."

"I can't either. But she has a therapist who had a similar experience and knows what it was like for her. So that's helpful."

"Most of the time we don't even know the kids are missing," Frank said, "and when we do know they're missing, most of the time we don't find them, and when we do find them, most of the time they have no one to help them."

"Are you saying Amanda was lucky?"

"She wasn't lucky to be kidnapped and made a sex slave. That shouldn't happen to anyone. But she was lucky to have you and Brian as her parents."

"I hope you're right. We're going to do everything we can."

"My prayers are with you," Frank told her.

On Thursday they saw Heather again, on Friday they played tennis again, and on Saturday they worked in the yard as a family, the children raking leftover leaves and Brian trimming the hedges. She pulled up the ivy that was encroaching on the myrtle.

On Sunday they went to church together. They sat in their usual place, with Carol going into the pew first and Amanda with Bo and Matthew and Brian following her. She noticed that Amanda genuflected, and she wondered if Amanda remembered to do it or if she was simply imitating her mother. Amanda missed a few responses, but everyone was still getting used to the changes, and some people were still responding: "And also with you" instead of "And with your spirit." And no one but the choir could sing the new version of the Gloria.

When it came time for the Lord's Prayer Amanda was silent at the beginning, but she joined them when they prayed: "And give us this day our daily bread." At the sign of peace Amanda came into her arms like a lamb with Bo mashed between them.

Kneeling after Communion, Carol automatically thanked God for the rescue of Amanda, but then she wondered if she could believe in a God that allowed such things to happen to children. And she was leaning more toward doubt than faith.

On the way out she steered her family around the people who were lined up to talk to the priest, not knowing what she would say to him.

She had invited her parents for dinner after church, and when they arrived the kids were upstairs playing on their computers, so she had to call them and get them to come down and say hello to their grandparents. She didn't expect them to hang around while the adults had drinks and talked about things that bored kids, and she was willing to let them go back to their rooms until dinner was ready, but she did expect them to come down and say hello, and when she had to call them again she raised her voice.

"We hear you, mom," Matthew yelled back. "We'll be there in a second."

Softened by the implication that they were doing something together, she said: "Okay."

Her mother was already in the kitchen, inspecting the dish of lasagna that was about to go into the oven. Her mother asked: "Is there sausage in it?"

"Yeah," Carol said, feeling as if she had avoided a demerit. "There's also ground beef in it."

Her mother nodded approvingly. "You could put some more grated cheese on it."

She was cranking the grater over the lasagna when her kids came running into the kitchen, Matthew first and then Amanda.

"Hi, grandma," Matthew said, giving his grandmother a hug.

"Hi, Matthew," his grandmother said with her eyes on Amanda, who had stopped behind her brother as if she was waiting her turn.

Matthew stepped aside to let his sister pass, but Amanda hesitated, holding Bo against the side of her face. She finally came forward and hugged her grandmother.

"Hi, sweetie," her mother said. "I'm so glad to see you."

At that moment Brian and her father came into the kitchen.

"Hey, kids," her father said breezily as if nothing had happened. "How are you doing?"

"Hi, grandpa," Matthew said. "We're doing fine."

Amanda went right to her grandfather and hugged him.

"My little red-haired fox," her father crooned, holding his granddaughter tenderly.

Amanda relaxed in his embrace.

204

Amazed by her father, Carol had to smile. He was full of blarney, and there were times when he seemed oblivious of what was happening, but as she had learned from her own experiences of heartbreak he always knew what to say to a girl in distress.

While Brian got two bottles of beer out of the refrigerator Carol put the lasagna into the oven, and having made a dutiful appearance the kids went back upstairs.

She poured two glasses of white wine, and since everything was ready she joined her parents and her husband at the kitchen table. During the week she had talked with her mother on the phone, but until today she hadn't talked with her face to face since they had brought Amanda back from Japan, and she was anxious to hear what her mother had to say.

"She acts like she's five years younger," her mother said.

"In some respects she does," Carol agreed. "But in other respects she's where she was."

Her mother looked skeptical. "In what respects?"

"She plays tennis like she did before." As she said this she was conscious of the fact that there were now two periods in her daughter's life, before and after what had happened.

"In church she remembered the Lord's Prayer," Brian said.

"She looks the same to me," her father said.

"She's not the same," Carol said, believing her father was only staking out a position to stop them from going too far in their judgment of Amanda's condition.

"She'll never be the same," Brian said. "But I'm learning to accept that. And whatever she becomes, I'll always love her."

"Is she on drugs?" her mother asked after a silence.

"She's taking a drug for anxiety, but that's all. It won't hurt her, and maybe it'll help her."

"How do you know it won't hurt her?"

"I trust the doctor. She doesn't seem like a pill pusher."

"If we can drink alcohol," her father said, "she can take a drug for anxiety—unless you want her to start drinking alcohol."

Her mother gave him a dirty look. "What about Matthew? How's he handling it?"

"I think he's handling it well," Carol said. "He's very good with her."

"Well, I hope it doesn't affect him too much."

"I think it'll make him better and stronger."

"I think it will," Brian agreed. "In that respect he takes after his grandmother."

Her mother smiled, saying: "Flattery will get you nowhere."

On Monday afternoon she was sitting at the kitchen table with Amanda, working on a reading assignment from one of the books that Heather had given her, when the doorbell rang.

"I'll get it," she said. "Now, read that question and think about it. Okay?"

"Okay," Amanda said, gazing blankly at the page.

When she opened the door she saw it was Jimmy, who had a bundle of mail for her.

"Here, Mrs. Delaney," he said, handing it to her.

"Thank you, Jimmy. Are we getting personal delivery of our mail now?"

"Yeah, sure. But I wanted to ask you something." He paused. "You know where they have garden plots in Zinsser Park? Well, my dad got me a plot for this summer, so I can grow flowers and vegetables. My therapist thinks it would be good for me."

"It sounds like a good idea," she said, unable to guess where he was going with this.

"I know what happened to Amanda," he said. "My parents told me. I mean, they told me as much as they know. And when I saw her last week I could tell it was like what happened to me. So I've been thinking, and I've decided that if having a garden would be good for me, it would be good for Amanda."

"Are you saying we should get her a plot at Zinsser?"

"No, I'm offering to share my plot with her."

"What a nice thought, Jimmy."

"You think she'd want to do that?"

"I think she would. But why don't you go and ask her. She's in the kitchen."

He nodded. "Okay. You don't think people will mind if their mail's a little late today?"

"No, they won't mind. Don't worry." She stepped aside to let Jimmy in, and then she went out to wait on the porch so they would have complete privacy.

About five minutes later he reappeared with a smile on his face. "She wants to do it. We're going to start this Saturday. We have to clear the plot and get it ready for planting."

"Thank you," she said, touching his shoulder.

"I think it'll be good for both us," he said hopefully. "Well, I better go and deliver the mail. People might wonder what happened to me."

On Wednesday afternoon the UPS truck stopped in front of their house and the driver brought a package. Guessing what it was, she took the package into the kitchen, where Amanda was eating ice cream, and she found the paring knife she used to open packages.

"What is it?" Amanda asked as if she had no idea.

"Let's see." She opened the package and took out a box, which contained the phone. "It's for you."

Amanda stopped eating and watched while Carol took the phone out of the box.

"Is this the right model?" Carol asked, showing it to her.

"I think it is," Amanda said, taking it. She inspected it, and then she jumped as if someone had jabbed her in the back.

"Are you okay?"

Amanda set the phone on the table and gazed at it, frowning. Then incongruously she said: "We have to mark it so I'll know it's mine."

"Then go upstairs and get my nail polish," Carol told her.

"Okay," Amanda said, springing off the chair and leaving the phone on the table.

While she waited for Amanda to come back Carol wondered if seeing the phone had triggered something, but adhering to

Heather's plan to proceed carefully, she decided not to ask Amanda what had made her jump.

Amanda put the dot of pink where it had been on the other phone, and she waited for the nail polish to dry before she picked up the phone and tried it.

Her fingers remembered what to do, and she sent a text message to her brother.

She waited impatiently, staring at the phone as if her life depended on getting a response.

Her behavior reassured Carol since it was perfectly normal—the lives of all the kids depended on getting responses to their text messages.

With a look of instant gratification Amanda said: "He says he's on his way home."

On Saturday morning Amanda got up early, and she was ready when Jimmy came to get her. She had gloves that Carol had bought for her to protect her hands from using tools to prepare the soil. The weather was unseasonably warm, so she didn't need a jacket or even a sweatshirt. She wore a tee-shirt that was just like the one Bo had except it was several sizes larger, and she took him with her—they looked like a pair of Jeter fans.

Zinsser Park was only a few blocks from their house, so they could walk there. Watching them go, Carol was mindful of the fact that it was the first time Amanda would be out of her sight since they had rescued her, and she knew what happened the last time she had taken her eyes off Amanda, but she trusted Jimmy as she had trusted him years ago to baby-sit her children. And as they turned into Maple Lane, she felt the relief of not having to worry about Amanda for a few hours.

Toward noon she wandered up to Zinsser to see how they were doing. She took the path that led up to the fields where the kids played football and baseball and the guys, including some members of the volunteer fire department, played softball. From the top of the hill she could look down at the garden plots, and she saw Jimmy and Amanda working and Bo sitting on a corner of the fence like a supervisor. Jimmy was turning the earth with a spade, and Amanda was breaking the clods with a hoe. They projected a feeling of collaborative purpose.

Standing in the warm sunlight, Carol envisioned the garden they would create together: the green shoots, the double leaves, the stems, the branches, the buds, and the flowers.

Birth, life, and loving care.

Acknowledgments

Special acknowledgments to Rachel Lloyd, the Polaris Project, Network for Peace through Dialogue, and other organizations whose mission is to stop sex slavery, rescue its victims, and rehabilitate them. Their work inspired me to write this novel.

BOOK CLUB GUIDE TO

Outside the Gate

Tom Milton

An introduction to *Outside the Gate*

Carol Delaney and her husband Brian have taken their twelve-year-old daughter Amanda and her best friend Stacy for spring break to an all-inclusive resort on a Caribbean island. In the afternoon of the third day of their vacation they leave the girls on a tennis court after giving them permission to play one more set, and they return to their room for showers. They have no reason to worry about the girls, who are being watched by the tennis pro and can get anything they want—from sodas and snacks to computer games—inside the resort.

A half hour later Carol goes to the girls' room, which is next to hers, and tries to rouse them. When they don't respond she calls Amanda on her cell phone, but the call fails. After looking for the girls everywhere inside the resort and not finding them, Carol and Brian learn from a boy who was washing a car in the parking lot that the girls snuck out, evidently wanting to explore the island. Accompanied by the boy and a security guard, the parents go after the girls in a golf cart, following their route into town, stopping at an ice cream store, and continuing to the harbor. The girls are nowhere in sight, but the boy spots a cell phone in the brush. It belongs to Amanda, and it looks as if it was stomped on by a heavy foot.

The security guard calls the police, who arrive immediately. After talking with two fishermen who were coming into the harbor as a yacht was going out, the police believe that the girls were abducted by Russians who live on the island and conduct business from a house they built there. Among other activities the police believe that the Russians are involved in human trafficking. The case is assigned to a detective who requests the American ships that patrol the area for drug smugglers to search for the yacht and detain it. Meanwhile, the police conduct a thorough search of the island in the hope that the girls escaped from the kidnappers and are hiding somewhere. A few hours later Carol and Brian learn that an American ship found the yacht but the girls were not on it. The detective still believes that the girls were abducted by the Russians, who must have transferred them to another boat. But when the police search the yacht after it returns to the harbor they find no evidence that the girls were on it, so they have no cause to arrest the Russians.

The next day Stacy's parents arrive, and her father, a lawyer who looks down on the island police, attempts to get the U.S. government to put pressure on the island government to arrest the Russians and make them talk. But his efforts backfire when the fishermen, who must have been threatened, retract their story about passing the yacht on their way into the harbor. By then the police have determined that the girls are not on the island, and since nothing more can be done there, the parents fly home.

At the first opportunity they meet with the FBI, which has joined the investigation, and they appear on television in order to publicize the kidnapping and extend the network of people who are aware of it. Though they don't have that kind of money, they offer a reward of a million dollars for information that enables them to find the girls.

A few days later they learn that Stacy has escaped from the kidnappers in Panama. Since she will be able to identify the men who abducted her, the police will then be able to arrest them and find out where they took Amanda. But the day after they bring Stacy home her parents receive a phone call from the kidnappers who threaten to kill both their children if Stacy identifies them, and Carol and Brian are unable to convince them to let Stacy talk with the FBI, though she has information that could save Amanda.

Following the advice of a colleague at work Carol contacts a nongovernmental organization whose mission is to rescue victims of human trafficking, and they refer her to a private detective who works with them. But time is running out for Amanda since every day it becomes more likely that she will be irreversibly damaged if she is put to work as a sex slave.

A conversation with Tom Milton

You raised the issue of children being exploited for commercial sex in your novel Infamy. *In our conversation about that novel you pointed out the many ways the girls on the street were exploited, not only for sex. In this novel you focus on the issue of children being forced into sex slavery. What made you write about this issue?*

I've been aware of it for a long time, but about five years ago I was deeply troubled when I saw girls who looked like they were twelve years old on the streets of Madrid selling their bodies. I put that feeling into *Infamy* in the character of a former cop whose mission was to protect the girls and ultimately liberate them from "the life," as they call it. But the feeling didn't go away.

Did you encounter the issue again?

Yes. In the town where I live in the Dominican Republic, I saw girls who weren't old enough to go to high school offering their bodies to tourists. And what finally made me realize that they were victims of modern slavery was a speaker I heard at a conference on the subject. Her name is Rachel Lloyd, and drawing on her own experience she told us how girls get enslaved and what happens to them. It was the first time I heard the terms "sex slavery" and "modern slavery." Since then I've been reading about it, starting with Rachel Lloyd's book *Girls Like Us,* and I've gotten involved with organizations whose mission is to stop sex slavery, rescue its victims, and rehabilitate them.

Clearly, a reason for writing this novel was to raise awareness of the issue.

Raising awareness of social issues is a reason for writing all my novels.

But it's not your only reason.

No. I also write to tell stories and reveal the inner conflicts of people.

In this novel your main character is a mother whose child gets kidnapped by human traffickers. Other writers have used this situation, but you used it not only to raise awareness of the issue but also to reveal the conflict of a woman who wanted her children to grow up in a better neighborhood than she did and then realizes that she might have put her children at risk by sheltering them from things that happen "outside the gate."

This conflict arises when parents try to insulate their children from what happens in the real world. Though they may not live in communities that are literally gated, their children are sheltered in a number of ways. Instead of freely roaming the neighborhood and randomly encountering people, their children are driven to scheduled events and play dates, where they encounter people who are demographically like them.

So their children don't know about the real world.

They don't know as much about the real world as children who live outside the gate.

One of your characters in The Golden Door *comments that America is turning into a gated community. He's referring to our immigration laws and the attitudes of many people in this country toward immigrants. Do you think our whole country is trying to insulate itself from what happens in the real world?*

I think it is. We've always had isolationist tendencies, which rise and fall in cycles, but now I think we're in an up cycle, especially after two disastrous wars.

I was just thinking that through the internet children have access to a lot of information even if they live in gated communities. Doesn't this enable them to learn about the real world?

They have access to a virtual world that has been created to entertain them. It's not the real world. And what troubles me is the extent to which they confuse the virtual world with the real world. They may not know the difference between killing people with electronic bullets and killing them with real bullets in classrooms or movie theaters.

You're a college teacher. You're dealing with young people who grew up in the virtual world. How do you get them to deal with reality?

I have them talk with each other face to face. They spend the whole class talking with each other face to face, not sending text messages to each other or to people they've met in the virtual world. And you know what? They like it.

Maybe they like the novelty of it.

Maybe they recognize the limitations of the virtual world. If you think about it, the internet is an aggregator, meaning that it brings together things and people of a similar nature. So it's actually doing the same thing parents do by raising their children in "gated" communities—it's limiting their experience with the diversity of the real world.

Going back to your story, I noticed that as usual your characters get into situations where their values are tested. I especially liked the situation that arises when one of the girls escapes from the kidnappers. Her mother knows they can save the girl who is still in captivity, but the kidnappers have threatened to kill both her daughters if she lets her daughter talk with the FBI. To say the least, it's an excruciating dilemma.

It is, and it's easy to judge her if you're not in her situation.

Would that apply to any situation?

I think it would. It's always easier to judge people if you're not in their situation. That's because we have trouble imagining ourselves in other people's situations.

Your main character, Carol, the mother of the girl who is still in captivity, tries to imagine herself in the other woman's situation.

She does try. But she doesn't really understand what it's like to be in that situation until she's in a similar situation herself.

So in this respect are we limited by our imaginations?

I think we are. I mean, Carol couldn't imagine what happens to her child. Yet it happens to other people's children every day.

I assume that's why you made this victim of human trafficking the daughter of happily married parents who love their children, as opposed to the more typical victims.

I want people to realize that it could happen to anyone.

There's a current of blame running through the story, which twists and turns and keeps revealing another side of things. And I have the feeling that you want your characters to end up taking their fair shares of responsibility.

I do. And I want my readers to join them in taking their fair shares of responsibility for the fact that in the world today millions of children are in sex slavery.

Discussion questions

1. When the girls go missing Carol blames herself for taking her eyes off them. Is she being fair to herself?

2. Carol is inclined to believe that the girls would not have left the resort on their own if they had grown up in a neighborhood like the one she grew up in. What do you think?

3. Carol sees her children relying on the internet as a source of knowledge instead of asking their parents questions. Is this a generational problem?

4. Before reading this novel, to what extent were you aware of human trafficking?

5. Is there anything Carol could have done differently to prevent her daughter from being a victim of human trafficking?

6. The professionals in this novel who deal with human trafficking believe that governments have an interest in it. What do you believe?

7. How does Amanda differ from a typical victim of human trafficking?

8. Why did the author write about Amanda instead of a typical victim of human trafficking?

9. What do you think Carol learned from the experience of having her daughter trafficked?

10. Is there a solution to the problem of human trafficking?

11. The plot makes a link between the disorder suffered by a trafficked child and the disorder suffered by a deployed soldier. Is the link valid?

12. Carol believes that if she had been in Donna's position she would have let her daughter talk with the FBI. Do you think she would have?

13. If you had been in Donna's position, what would you have done?

14. Do you think Carol and Donna will ever be friends again? What about Amanda and Stacy?

15. What role does modern communications technology play in the plot of this novel?

16. If there is a hero in this novel, who is it?

17. What thoughts or feelings do you have about the ending?

CPSIA information can be obtained at www.ICGtesting.com
Printed in the USA
BVOW011123210213

313765BV00001B/1/P